JUNE DRUMMOND

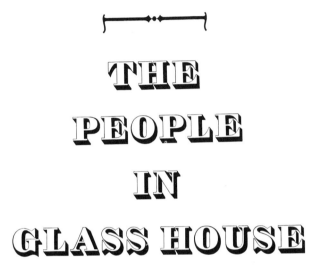

THE PEOPLE IN GLASS HOUSE

An Inner Sanctum Mystery

SIMON AND SCHUSTER
NEW YORK

"WHERE'S ADAM?"

"Stargazing."

"This night of all nights?"

"It's perfect, my dear, up there on the roof."

"I despair of him."

"Shall I fetch him down for you?"

"No. Leave him. There's time yet."

Perfect. Perfect.

Adam Villiers knew that he could not in the span of life hope for many nights as good as this.

It was the cold that had done it, an immaculate finger of cold that touched London, extinguishing the smoke, tamping down the mist, sweeping one huge and glittering span from the frozen earth to the eons beyond the Galaxy.

He leaned his elbows on the parapet and breathed in this fiery air with gratitude. Twenty-six floors down, the Thames threw a thick black coil round the thrust of Southwark. From the encrusted glare of its banks distilled a thin singing, ships and traffic, water and the ring of metal.

He turned his head to look along the flank of the building. Glass House, people already called it that, with mockery and with awe. They came to stare at the milk-white curve of the front elevation, ignorant of the technical skills that had created it, yet acknowledging the power of glass, its strength and flexibility and adamantine grace.

It was necessary, the first principle, to create a market. Hand and eye must yearn, "give me, I want!" Was the ignorance necessary too? Must the creator withhold the secrets of creation, guarding his claim to be the one true source? Hardly. The finished product was inert, a certain arrangement of line and colour that any reasonably clever team could analyse and duplicate. The only mystery in industrial production, the only holy thing left, was life.

Then who, or what, breathed life into the Villiers Glass

Company? What made it a living membrane, vibrant in the tissue of the national economy? Where in twenty-six storeys of inert matter did the cell first quicken?

On the ground floor, perhaps, the display halls where the strolling crowds saw and coveted various objects, ovenware and surf-boats, chandeliers and laboratory equipment? Did birth begin with the first prickings of lust, the sparkle in the public eye?

Unlikely. That lust was deliberately inspired by the serpents in Derbyshire, Surrey and Norfolk. On seventeen factory sites the chemists and artists sweated, sketched and blew, mixed and moulded, annealed and ground and spun, evolving the forms that would ensnare an increasing number of consumers next year and the next.

Did life begin when the specifications reached Planning on the middle floors of Glass House? In that case, Villiers Glass was no child of love. The warfare of the junior executives was relentless, Finance against Sales, Production against Advertising. Their acrimony tainted the air like the stink of cordite.

Nor was the air much purer in the upper strata. The emotions were more rarified, but still lethal. Behind the doors of Finance, Market Research, Import-Export and Legal Arm, one met a horn-rimmed, silk-lined opportunism. Instead of open striving, one had to deal with the subtle deploy of private means, the sly application of secret knowledge.

Nothing touched the hearts in the Board Room on level twenty-three, except an occasional coronary infraction.

Yet there was life in Villiers Glass. It must not be allowed to seep away, the finger must find the vital pressure point and grip there before the haemorrhage of talent proved fatal.

Life.

Somewhere on its journey the sand, limestone and soda ash became glass and more than glass, became the substance that served the national interest, that was essential to scientific and medical progress, that shone in men's minds as the symbol of enlightenment.

How?

How much was the legacy of the dead men, the dead men of Canterbury and Chartres, the more recent dead like grandfather Morgan Villiers who built reflector telescopes, and his brother Robert who spun a fortune from glass fibres?

How much must still be contributed by the living? What must be given now, what must be promised for the future, to keep glass alive?

Adam's eyes strayed across the façade directly beneath him. Over the Board Room the building narrowed to an asymmetric pinnacle like the tower of an iceberg. This housed four of the senior directors of the Villiers Glass Company.

On the twenty-fourth floor were two flats; that of Adam, and that of Zoe Corelli. They shared a garden on the east side, with a patio, lawns, a small swimming-pool.

The floor above belonged to Walter Kepple, Financial Director. His garden lay to the west.

On the twenty-sixth floor with a view of all London, lived Grace Villiers, widow of the late Henry Villiers, mother of Adam, due in the coming week to relinquish to him the Presidency of the Company.

Her apartment contained the private library and art collection of the Villiers family. In the garden on the north side, under sheets of Villiers glass, grew magnolia trees, oranges and lemons and butterfly orchids.

Adam straightened his back, tilted his head until he could see the constellation Orion blazing towards its height. Betelgeux, Rigel, Mintaka, Alnilam, Alnitak. The light of Rigel, travelling at a speed of 186,000 miles a second, had taken at least five hundred and forty years to reach Earth. One could say that that glittering point in the sky was a link with the year 1428. The making of the great rose windows, the making of the 200-inch Hale Reflector for the Mount Palomar observatory, fell in the span of time covered by one blink of a star.

He bent forward, dizzy with the pressure of space. Far below him wheeled and spun the river, the streets, and the blank disc of the parking-ground. Light lay there in concentric swatches, and across the light a woman moved.

Adam watched her. She was dark-haired, wearing a bulky white coat. Both her arms were wrapped round a large oblong package. She came on with a steady, almost implacable gait until she was directly below where he stood; and there she halted and stared about her. He saw the white oval of her face turning in some mute question.

He leaned further out. Suddenly it seemed vital that he answer her. She was humanity, striding without fear under the fearsome stars, and he felt for her a quite ridiculous sense of kinship. He raised his arm and shouted, once and then again.

She did not look at him. Perhaps she did not hear. She started forward and vanished under the arcade that sheltered the display windows. He waited and watched for some time, but she did not re-appear.

II

"He's in the clouds."

Grace Villiers pressed a switch and the blue and silver filaments of a ten-foot Christmas tree shuddered with light. She put out a hand and exerted a gentle pressure on one of the branches, released it and said, "Not enough resilience, you see?"

The man on the sofa sat without moving. Feet widespread, arms outflung, he appeared to be studying the ceiling with close attention. Grace went across and stood before him, almost between his feet.

"Wally?"

He raised his head and looked at her. His eyes were opaque blue. They expressed, in contrast to his apparent immobility, a constant wariness. Thick auburn hair curled over his head and on the backs of his hands and wrists. His ears were small, flat and delicate, his chin deeply cleft. There was in his pose an odd mixture of brute vigour and feminine grace. He looked like a figure on a Cretan vase, a bull-dancer whose sole weapon was his speed of body and mind. He said in a sharp, staccato voice:

"You talking about Adam, or that tree?"

He watched her face sharpen in the animosity that these days so easily became savage. It was a pity, he thought, that she was such a tricky bitch. He kept his gaze on her, staring her down, and after a moment she lifted her shoulders in a shrug.

"Both, I suppose."

"You ask too much of both. Glass is glass. Adam is Adam. Don't put too much strain on either and we'll get by."

She stepped over his outstretched leg and sat on the sofa, half-facing him.

"I ask no more than is necessary. Unless Adam can carry an exceptional weight, this whole move is pointless."

Kepple was silent and she raised her voice. "Well? Do you think it's easy to take over the presidential chair at the age of thirty-three?"

"You were only thirty."

"Entirely different. I'd been President in effect for years before Henry died."

"Don't worry. You've done the right thing about Adam."

"I've done the only thing possible. I meant to hold office until Adam was forty; but we must have continuity of control over the next three years, and I can't promise that. I saw Fraser last month. The tests showed deterioration."

"I know." His right hand moved suddenly, the fingers lightly caressing her shoulder.

"Who told you?"

He shook his head and she smiled. "Not much you don't know about me, is there, Wally?"

"You'll live to be a hundred."

"Perhaps." Her eyes went back to the tree. "I wish I could be sure of him. I wish I knew what went on in his head."

"The point is," Kepple turned his hand impatiently, "Adam has a head. He is capable of thought. He's been learning the job since he was seventeen, he's worked with all our best men, he's been on the best managerial courses, he knows glass, he's got the family name to help him along. The Board supports his nomination, and in February at the A.G.M. he'll duly be elected President. What more do you want?"

"I want," she said slowly, "whatever is more than enough. Villiers is dynastic. Adam must rule an Empire."

"Vive l'Empereur!"

"Exactly, and I understand better than you how hard it is

to survive. One must excel. Can Adam do that? Can he out-manoeuvre the cabals, can he act alone in a crisis, can he coax that damn Board into agreeing on the simplest matter? I don't know. I don't really know what he is, I'm too close to him. What frightens me is that the vote was so narrow. He wouldn't have made it without Matt's support. And why did Matt back him? Because he really thought Adam was the right man, or because he felt a sense of loyalty to Henry?"

"I would remind you that I too knew Henry in the days of our youth." Kepple pulled himself upright. His irritable gaze flickered over the woman beside him, over the twist of grey-gold hair, the fragility of collarbone, the silky tautness of the deltoid muscles, the too-thin, elegant hands. "I knew him and considered him a half-witted creep. That didn't antagonise my vote. It went for Adam."

"Why?"

"Your interest, my darling, is a little belated. I take it my opinion is of less moment than Matt's?"

"Don't be absurd. It's simply a question of the diversity of your influence. Yours is deep, but narrow. What you think counts with Finance. Matt's opinion counts with the factories, with Planning, most of Production lines up behind him."

"Matt, in a word, makes friends while I make enemies?"

"Yes," she said coolly, "that's true in a sense. You didn't come up from the Works. You've no feeling for labour, in fact you don't care for people at all. That doesn't bother me. You weren't hired to be one of the boys." Leaning forward, she took his right wrist in her fingers. "You're a smart, educated cut-throat, indispensable to me and to this Company. You have the best financial brain in the trade. I can trust you to reach an unemotional decision. That is why your vote means more to me than all the rest put together, because it's cast without emotion."

He stared at her, still angry. "My darling Grace, don't make that mistake. There was plenty of emotion in my vote. Don't think I see Adam as a white hope. I don't. I voted for him because that was the only way to prevent an election from outside the Company ranks. I voted for him because he's the only man we can guide the way we want him to go. Adam is going to take his line from you, from me, and from Matt. So don't let's have any more bull about whether or not he's fit to run the show. He's not going to be allowed to run it. I don't give a darn about how he feels about the Presidency. I don't even think it's relevant. We are going to push through our expansion programme and not even your white-headed boy is going to interfere."

She sat looking at him for some moments, then said, "Don't be too arrogant, Wally. He might surprise you."

"Perhaps."

"He's my son."

"A point in his favour. And Henry's, a point against."

She was about to make some retort when a buzzer sounded some distance off in the hall. Above the gilt doors of the elevator, a Lalique panel sprang into soft rose light.

"That will be Matt. Will you fetch Adam down now, please?"

Kepple hesitated, then got up without looking at her and moved towards the stairway at the far end of the room.

III

THE MAN STEPPING out of the lift was uglier than an Aztec war-mask. His frame was vast, his limbs gnarled, his paunch formidable. A crop of grizzled hair made his skull look like an outsize pot-scourer, and his nose was frankly Cyranic.

Matt Kinsman's adversaries sometimes complained that his ugliness gave him an unfair advantage. On the occasions when he appeared on television, viewers marvelled at the strange topography of his face; yet found it immensely attractive. The common touch, charisma, whatever describes the ability to evoke a sympathetic response, Matt possessed.

Now, as he lumbered towards the woman on the sofa, his little black eyes sharpened in concern. He bent and kissed her on the cheek, straightened and stared down at her.

"Now who said what to make you look like that?"

She answered quickly, almost without thought. "Wally says Adam is like Henry."

Matt glanced towards the stairway, back at Grace. "So he is, in some ways. No harm in that."

"Can he fill the Presidency?"

"He wants to."

"That's not the question."

But, thought Matt, it is the question, the only one. Once, long ago when he and Henry first started in the factory, he had wanted to learn to roll the blowing-irons. Later, he'd wanted to be foreman, to be works manager, to be Director of Production.

There had been a point when he might have taken over the whole of Villiers Glass . . . had he wanted to.

That was when old Morgan Villiers died of virus pneumonia. Everyone said Henry was unfit to step into the old man's shoes. True too, in some ways. Henry was an artist, a brilliant designer, but too erratic to be a systems man. Too shy to handle labour. Nervous even with people he'd known for years. Ill half the time. Every winter, the asthma was worse. And married to Grace Upton, who was rich and beautiful and clever and had the knack of making her husband as miserable as hell.

So there was the Villiers family controlling the Company; and about fifty people aiming to control Henry. A week after the funeral the first clique started to build up. Some of the older directors had broken that up, come to Matt and offered him the chair.

Instead, he'd picked his own candidate. Henry. And backed Henry with two new directors. One was a clever, sullen young man from the costing department, name of Walter Kepple. The other was Grace.

And they'd done none too badly. Re-shaped the whole of Villiers Glass in those pre-war years. Brought in employment and training reforms, switched four factories on to new lines, lenses and laboratory equipment. The refugee experts from Germany and Czechoslovakia had helped. They'd built up the transport fleets and acquired new sites. This site, for Glass House, was bought in 1935.

Between them, they'd compensated for Henry's shortcomings. Felt pretty proud of themselves, poor silly sods. Got what

12

they wanted.

The second time, though, was different. When Henry died in 1939 and they offered him the presidency, he'd refused it. Some of them said right out he hadn't the guts to take the top job. That wasn't so. He wanted it all right, but he had to think of Adam. Difficult to explain, but he'd known that for Adam to grow up with a mind of his own, Grace had to be occupied elsewhere. She'd wanted the presidency, it could give her what she needed and leave the boy free. He let her take it.

Twenty years later when Glass House was being built, Grace urged him to have one of the top-floor apartments. He'd told her bluntly he didn't fancy living over the shop.

She'd been astonished and hurt. "What nonsense, you've slept in a factory before now!"

"When I had to, during the war. There's a peace on now, love. I don't like spending my leisure with my work-mates, and I don't want to be where any boy with gripes can corner me after hours."

"I need you near me. You're one of the family."

"That I'm not!"

"Adam depends on you."

"Adam will find me at my desk during the day, and from seven at night he can reach me at 3, Bridehead Road, The Paragon."

"Is it that you don't want to live near Wally?"

"What gave you that daft idea?"

"You don't approve of him and me."

"It's none of my business if you let Kepple nip up your back stairs. Seems though it'd make things easier for Adam if you took a husband instead of a fancy man. Why don't you marry Wally?"

"I don't choose to."

"Still don't trust him, do you, girl?"

"If I married Wally, he'd force me out of the presidency. Much as I'd like a regular existence, I must put Adam first. I am acting regent for him. Everything I do, I do for Adam."

"Well, I don't want your attic floor, Grace. I prefer to keep both feet on the ground."

And he continued to live in his comfortable old home at Blackheath.

Not that he neglected that tiny inner ring that Grace counted as her family. He often dined at Glass House, he shared with its tenants all important festivals and anniversaries. But Blackheath was his own place, and there Adam could find sanctuary.

As the years passed, this became increasingly important. Grace had always been formidable. It took a resolute man to resist her powerful mind, her beauty, her bone-deep knowledge that she was in the right. And now there was her illness. She faced it with great courage; but as her own body failed her, she was beginning to draw on the strength of others. Kepple could and would look after himself, but Adam was more vulnerable.

And now, for the third and last time, the presidency stood open, and he was refusing to claim it. This time he wanted it for Adam.

He thought with wry humour, everything I have not done, has been for Adam. But aloud he said to Grace, "I've always gone for the job I really wanted. Adam wants the presidency. He can fill it."

Grace got up then and moved restlessly about the room. She came to a halt before the Christmas tree. Matt crossed to her side.

"It's very nice."

Grace put out a finger and touched one of the branches. "I'm not happy. The fusing is weak here, you see? They must improve it before I pass it."

He bent to look at the anneal at the joints. "I think you're being too fussy. Hoppners only want the things for window-dressing, not for public sale. If you increase the strength, you'll price it out of their reach."

"I won't pass shoddy design."

And that, thought Matt, was going to be Adam's first problem, how to get round her relentless search for perfection. Grace was never satisfied. Nothing was good enough. Twenty years ago, that was fine. People wanted what they bought to last a lifetime. Now they didn't. Housewives couldn't afford hand-cut crystal and blown glass, they wanted a bit of bright stuff that looked good on a white Swedish table. And Hoppners Stores wanted a new window display every year. Grace was right in one way, of course, they'd be putting Villiers Glass on display in shops right across the country, the tree must be good enough to show people that glass was better than plastic, more vibrant and alive. But the tree could do that well enough the way it was. No need to waste time on such a trivial thing.

Grace was too proud. Pride had lost her Henry, and it would lose her Adam too if she didn't watch out.

Matt looked at her sadly and with love, seeing Adam in her. Same light hair and brows, same bones that gave a gleam to the skin on cheeks and forehead. Like lead crystal, both of them, sharp-cut and full of light. But Adam sometimes threw out a surprise flash. Was it from Henry that he had that odd glint? And was it humour, or a flaw, an uncertainty in his make-up?

Matt put an arm round Grace's shoulders. "Don't fret about anything tonight. It's Christmas, we've got three weeks' holiday, let's have a bit of fun."

She went with him to the far end of the room where drinks had been set out. By long custom, all the servants of the Glass House flats had gone off duty from Christmas Night until the day after Boxing Day, but there were snacks arranged on the bar and champagne cocktails waiting in its built-in refrigerator. Matt accepted one of these although he would have preferred whisky. As he lifted the glass, voices sounded on the staircase and Kepple and Adam came down into the room.

The young man came straight over to greet Matt. The cold air of the roof clung to his clothes like an aura, and his face was ruddy.

Matt smiled up at him. "A splendid night."

"Wonderful."

"Bloody perishing," said Kepple. His features were pinched and irritable. He took a champagne glass in both hands and sipped. "Where's Zoe? Can't we eat, I'm ravenous?"

Grace said soothingly, "She'll be up as soon as she can.

She only got back from France an hour ago. She's exhausted."

But when Zoe Corelli burst from the elevator ten minutes later, she looked anything but exhausted. She shot towards them, saucer-eyed, thin hands flapping.

"Grace, everyone, you must come at once, we've got to clear the building. Someone's planted a bomb in the foyer."

"A bomb!" Kepple started to laugh and Zoe screamed at him, stamping both feet like a child.

"Hurry, can't you? Cartwright 'phoned me and said we must get out at once. Don't just stand there sniggering."

At her words, the wailing of the fire alarms filled the labyrinths below them. They ran to the lift, Adam with his arm round Grace, Kepple still clutching his champagne glass with its sugar-coated rim.

IV

"SORRY, MR. VILLIERS, but I couldn't take any chances."

Cartwright the caretaker was waiting for them by the elevator doors at the rear of the building. The skirts of his brand-new overcoat shone greenish in the neon lighting. His square face was both anxious and apologetic.

"It's maybe just a silly joke, sir." He pointed along the arcade that led to the front foyer. "That's it there, that red box. It's been fixed to the main display window with masking-tape."

Kepple said sharply, "That's the Italian Loan glass."

"Not now," said Matt. "It was moved out yesterday."

"But that's what bothered me, Mr. Kinsman." The caretaker rubbed fingers against thumbs. "It could be someone thought the loan glass was still in the showroom. So I've rung the police. They'll be here any minute."

"Is there anyone else in the building?" asked Grace.

"No, Madam. All the offices closed early yesterday on account of Christmas. The desk checked everyone out, and the fire-doors are locked on each level. I've switched on the buzzers in case, but I'm certain nobody's up there. And the last ten minutes I've been standing within sight of the back foyer.

I rang Mrs. Corelli from my flat."

"You saw no-one hanging about?" said Matt.

"Not a soul. I'd just done the round of the building and when I reached the front foyer, I spotted the box. I came back here, 'phoned the police, 'phoned Mrs. Corelli."

"It may be a decoy," said Kepple, "to get us out of our apartments. I think we ought to watch both the entrances."

"That's right," said Matt, "cops and robbers. Wally, you stay here at the back with Cartwright. Adam and I will nip round to the front. The women had best stay here."

Grace said, "I shall come with you."

Zoe snatched at her arm. "Don't be mad. You mustn't go near that thing, you'll be killed."

"My dear Zoe, it's either a silly hoax, or an attempt to burgle my flat. I want to know which."

"It's a bomb, I tell you. It's got a fuse, a long fuse, you can see it."

"You stay here with Wally, then."

"But I want to be with you, Grace. Oh, why is everyone so stupid?" Complaining in a steady whine, Zoe trotted after Grace and the two men. They circled the building, taking the road that ran round the west side of Glass House. The cold was like a hammer and Grace shivered in her evening dress. Adam took off his jacket and wrapped it round her shoulders. She lifted her face to stare at the pearly walls above them and said in a low voice, "Could it really be a bomb? Why would anyone do that?"

"Some beat's idea of a joke, perhaps."

They reached the parking ground as a police car swung through the main gates. The vehicle shot towards them and checked neatly some fifty yards from the building. Men jumped out, two policemen and a soldier in khaki. The soldier hefted a box from the boot. One of the policemen sprinted away along the side road. The other approached Matt.

"Sergeant Innes, sir. Are you Mr. Villiers?"

Silently Matt indicated Adam. The policeman's gaze shifted wearily. "It was your caretaker, then, name of Cartwright, who 'phoned and reported a suspected bomb-plant?"

"Yes," said Adam. "It's over there."

He walked towards the building with Innes. The soldier with the box fell in behind them. At the main doors, Adam halted.

"There it is."

They faced a huge crystalline hall, lit by a modern chandelier of coloured stalactites. On the right stretched reception desks, kiosks, the front elevators. On the left were the display windows. Taped against the biggest of these was a bright red cylinder some two feet long, decorated with clusters of red ribbon. A white fuse ran from the far end of the cylinder to a small square box on the floor.

Innes said sharply, "Who are those people?" and Adam glanced along the arcade to the distant figures by the rear elevators.

"Walter Kepple, our Finance Director, and Cartwright who called you in. We thought someone had better watch the back door." As he spoke, the second policeman came into view, and they saw Kepple turn and address him. Innes grunted and waved the soldier forward.

"You'd better get cracking. Can I help?"

"No." The soldier stepped delicately across the foyer. Innes and Adam watched through the glass doors.

Adam said, "Do you usually call in the Army?"

Innes answered without turning his head, "You've got a valuable loan here, sir. We try to keep an eye on such things. Tell me, why did your man call us before he spoke to you?"

Adam shrugged. "Instructions. In any emergency, call the police first. Incidentally, the Italian Loan left that window yesterday. It's in the vaults, ready for shipment."

"Umh. What would it take to break the window?"

"Bullets, nothing less."

"And the rear casing?"

"The same."

"Had any threats? Any suggestion that someone might pull this stunt?"

"No."

"You'd have been told, I take it?" Innes's eyes studied Adam, the unlined face, the thick hair untouched with grey.

Adam's mouth curled suddenly. "I think so. I'm running

for President of the Company."

Innes nodded. His gaze went back to the soldier in the foyer. The man was listening to the cylinder with some electronic device. As they watched he turned his head and they saw his face, blind, absorbed.

"Enjoying himself," said Adam.

"Bomb-disposal's his racket. Not mine, I'm getting old, bombs don't make me laugh any more." He glanced at his watch. "On Christmas Day, you'd think they'd give us a break, wouldn't you?"

"You get a lot of this sort of thing?"

"Too much. While we fiddle about here, someone may be in real trouble. On the other hand, if we ignore that box and it does explode . . . we can't win."

"There's something very unpleasant about a hoaxer."

"Mad. Malicious."

The young soldier stood up and turned towards the door, held up his hands in an angler's gesture, indicating a shrimp.

"He thinks it's safe to handle," said Innes.

"Mightn't it be a trembler device?"

"Have to trust his judgement, sir." Innes jerked his shoulders. "I suggest you move back a bit." He made no move himself however, and Adam stayed where he was.

"He's going to shift it."

Slowly, with great gentleness, the soldier peeled off the masking-tape, lowered the cylinder to the ground. Ten minutes later he had disconnected the fuse and disembowelled the smaller box. He picked something from the wreckage and brought it out to Adam.

"Your name Villiers?"

"Yes." Adam took the proffered envelope. It contained a card, about eight inches by six, and he turned it so that he could read it by the light of the display windows.

"Happy Christmas, Henry darling." The words were written in italic script. On the reverse side of the card was a scale drawing of what looked like a Christmas bauble, many-spoked, delicate as a snow-flake, painted red and gold. The colours were faded and the edges of the card slightly yellowed. In the bottom left-hand corner were the figures 183. Adam shook his head and handed the card to Innes.

Innes frowned at it. "Mean anything to you, sir?"

"Not a thing"

"Who's Henry?"

"My father, perhaps."

"He live here?"

"He died in 1939."

Innes stared blankly at Adam, then sighed. "All right. We'll take it and the envelope and check them. Don't expect we'll get anything useful."

Adam said, "There's been no crime, so far."

"No sir. But keep in touch. Any other trouble, tell us at once."

He turned away, raised his arm and beckoned the policeman at the far end of the arcade. Adam walked swiftly across to the soldier, who was busy with the main cylinder.

"What's inside?"

The young man grinned up at him. "Lot of straw, and this." He held up a stubby cardboard tube.

"What is it?"

"Roman Candle."

Adam stared at the firework. He thought of the woman he had seen crossing the parking-ground. She had carried a parcel. He wondered if the paper would show fingerprints.

He said to the soldier, "I think the Sergeant wants you." The man moved off. Adam carried the firework out to the middle of the clear ground. He set it down, took a box of matches from his pocket, struck a light and applied it to the twist of blue paper. It caught and he ran backwards, watching. There was a hissing sound, a burst of splendid magenta flame.

"Hey!" Innes was running to his side, hustling him towards the building. "You shouldn't have done that."

"It's just a firework."

"Yes, but . . ." Innes hunched his shoulders in final resignation. "All right. Forget it."

He began to pick up the scattered paper, the masking-tape and scrolls of red ribbon. Matt, Kepple, Grace and Zoe converged on the foyer, all talking at once.

Outside on the parking-ground the Roman Candle shot

into the air a red, a blue, and a brilliant gold star.

V

"IT's SPOILED MY whole Christmas," said Zoe. "Not that it started too well. The climax, in fact, of a perfectly bloody week."

"Put it out of your mind," said Grace. "It was only some crank." She piled the last of the plates on to a trolley. "Adam, would you take this out, and bring back the coffee? It's all ready on the tray. Matt, dear, would you look after the liqueurs?"

The men moved in obedience. Matt said, "Zoe, what for you?"

"Kirsch. Nothing French. I'm off the French."

"For interest," said Wally with false sweetness, "how did your talks go?"

"They'll take the Tycoon designs, but not the Jet Set."

"Tycoon was Koch, wasn't it? And Jet Set your own?"

Zoe said nothing. Her scowl became more pronounced. She had a small pointed face that registered every emotion to excess. Her mode of speech was also exaggerated. She was like a child, posturing and mouthing through a piece of elocution. People sometimes made the mistake of thinking she was a mere puppet, but she was by no means ineffectual. Her nature was complex and deep. Even those who knew her best could not always be sure what motivated her actions.

She had been twice married and twice divorced, her first husband being a banker's son, her second a racing motorist. Neither union lasted longer than two years.

She was first cousin to Grace, had been brought up in the same household, gone to the same schools, and travelled south to share the same début and season. In the London of the nineteen-thirties she had proved something of a hit. She fitted the frenetic mood of the times; yet even while she moved in the smart and raffish society of her two husbands, she kept her eye on another world. She frequented artistic circles, developed her flair for design, built up useful friendships with figures in industry and commerce.

When Grace married Henry Villiers, Zoe's second marriage was crumbling, and she was extremely hard up. She joined the Villiers Company as a junior designer. By the time of Henry's defection, she had arrived at the head of the Design department, and when Grace became President, Zoe won her directorship.

Over the years, various competent and forthright executives had expressed doubts about her ability. Their jobs were filled in due course by men better acquainted with the ways of the world.

The wise knew that no-one outside the magic inner ring would oust Zoe Corelli. She was unpopular with her own staff, poison to the personnel officers, disliked by many clients; but she knew more about Grace Villiers than any living soul. Some said that Grace kept Zoe as one keeps a talisman, a luck-piece from the past. Perhaps Zoe herself had invented that tale.

Now she gave Walter Kepple an acid smile. "It's no good trying to change the subject, Wally. I want to know who planted that thing in the foyer, and why?"

Kepple shrugged. Grace said, "Some crank, no doubt, and for no valid reason."

"The police made complete sillies of themselves. That Sergeant never asked me a single question."

"He questioned Cartwright."

"Well, I don't think he took it seriously at all."

"I hope not."

"Goodness me, what a thing to say."

"Zoe, I certainly don't want the police pursuing me with questions. Imagine the nuisance, darling. Questions and formalities, I'd much sooner forget all about it. So would we all."

"I want to know," persisted Zoe. Adam came into the room with the coffee-tray, and she raised her voice petulantly. "Adam, what was in that box?"

"Boxes," said Adam, and Kepple looked up sharply.

"There was something in both?"

"Yes." Adam set the tray down carefully. "The big cylinder

held a Roman Candle . . ."

". . . Roman, you see?" Zoe took a swig of kirsch. She had already drunk a good deal of wine, and her nose and forehead shone. "Might well refer to the Italian Loan."

But Kepple interrupted impatiently. "And in the small box?"

"A card." Adam held up measuring fingers. "About this size. There was a sort of Christmas decoration painted on one side, and a message on the other."

"What message?"

Adam glanced at Grace. "It said, 'Happy Christmas, Henry darling.'"

For a moment there was complete silence, and in that pause fear brushed the room like the swift and dipping flight of a bat.

Kepple spoke first, stretching out his hand. "Can I see that?"

"I haven't got it, Wally. Sergeant Innes took it away with him."

"Why? No crime was committed."

"He mentioned tests. Perhaps there's some routine check for fingerprints or something."

Zoe's voice cut across them sharply. "Henry's dead. Nobody sends a Christmas card to a dead man. It's horrible, I don't understand it."

"Zoe, be quiet." Grace spoke with emphasis. "When will we get it back from the police, Adam?"

"I suppose in a day or two."

"When it arrives, give it to me and I will burn it. I want to forget the whole unpleasant little episode."

Matt shook his head. "No, Grace. You can't do that, love."

"Why not?"

"Because it's evidence. Adam, can you remember any other details?"

"The card was hand-drawn, not printed. The message was in italic script, fairly practised, I'd say. The edges of the card were yellow, so I imagine it's several years old."

"We'll have to take a good look at it. Perhaps we can have it tested by a hand-writing expert. It may even ring bells with one of us."

"I don't wish it to ring bells," said Grace with vigour. "It's a cruel practical joke by a diseased mind, and we should ignore it."

Matt sighed. "It's because it is cruel that we can't ignore it, don't you see? Zoe's right. Nobody sends a Christmas card to a dead man. It follows the card was meant for the living, for one of us, and whoever sent it didn't mean it kindly. We'll just have to sit tight and wait."

"For what?" said Zoe. "For his New Year greeting?"

Matt shrugged. "I doubt if this joker will wait that long."

VI

THE NEXT MORNING after breakfast, Adam left Glass House and drove down to Blackheath. He found Matt walking round his garden, a bacon-and-egg sandwich in one hand, an edger in the other. He said as Adam came up to him, "I thought you'd be round. What's your case?"

Adam sat down on a wheelbarrow full of sacks. "I saw a woman approaching Glass House last night. I was up on the roof and I saw her cross the parking area and head for the main arcade. She was carrying a big parcel."

"You think she planted the boxes?"

"It's possible."

"Why didn't you tell Innes?"

Adam turned up a palm and studied it. "At the time, I felt one must avoid a fuss. Thinking it over this morning, I decided I was right. This is a private matter. Isn't it?"

Matt finished his sandwich, planted the edger in the nearest flower-bed, and dusted his hands on the seat of his trousers. "We'd best talk inside."

He led the way to a small breakfast-room where a gas-fire burned. Sinking into a wing-chair and waving Adam to another he said flatly, "Now tell me. Have you been concealing anything else from the police? Any threatening letters, anything like that?"

"No. But I expect those will come. I think the bomb-scare was just the first move."

"Why? It could be an isolated prank. Some student perhaps."

"On Christmas night? And that woman didn't look like a student, or a crank for that matter. There was . . . I don't know . . . a sort of precision about her. She knew exactly what she was going to do."

"Well," Matt reached for a rack of pipes, chose one, and polished it absently on the side of his nose, "you can say so, but it's just guessing, my friend."

"We're meant to guess, aren't we?"

Matt's eyes became wary. "Perhaps."

"Matt, stop dodging the issue. You saw my mother's face last night. And I saw yours, let me remind you. That card business shook you rigid. If my father had walked into the room you couldn't have looked more shaken."

"Henry's ghost," said Matt slowly. "Maybe it was, at that."

"Why?"

"Henry's name on a Christmas card. He always thought a lot of Christmas. I suppose he's been on my mind this week. The change in the presidency, last time that happened was when Henry died, in 1939. I've been remembering him. We all have. So when you told us about the card, it kind of brought him right into the present, right into the room so to speak. Gave me a jolt, I'll admit."

"Wally too. He looked as nervous as a cat. You think he knows more than he's telling?"

"Wally always knows more than he tells."

"You think he knows who planted the card?"

"Wait a moment." Matt laid the pipe aside and wagged a forefinger. "Kepple doesn't fish for tiddlers. He's crafty, and he's tough, but he's not small. He wants to own Glass House and when the moment comes he'll do his best to have you out of the chair and himself in. But he won't indulge in tea-cup plotting, he's not that sort of fool. Wally knows exactly how far he can go at any given moment. Right now, he needs to keep in Grace's good books, so you take it from me he didn't know anything about that card. And since we're on the subject, I'll give you a word of advice. When he does move against you, he'll come in so fast you won't see what hits you. So watch him. Watch him, and use him for your own ends and the Company's ends. Bleed him of every pint of service he can supply. That's the code he understands. You can't exchange friendship or trust with the Kepples of this world; just mutual profit while the game lasts, then kill or be killed." Matt's long mouth quirked. "I repeat, I don't trust Wally, but I can't see him staging last night's little turn-up."

"And Zoe?"

"I thought last night she was scared. I don't think she knew anything about it."

"And my mother was taken completely by surprise. In other words, it was entirely an outside job." Adam leaned back, lacing his fingers behind his head. " 'Happy Christmas, Henry darling.' An old card, done by hand. I could show it around Glass House, perhaps one of the older employees might recognise it."

"Not a good way of keeping the thing to ourselves, is it?"

Adam got up and moved to the bay window. Outside, the morning had developed a rich blue patina that made the slopes of Blackheath glow like a Canaletto. He turned to face the old man in the wing chair.

"Everyone emphasises the need for privacy. Tell me something, Matt. Was there anything discreditable in my father's life, or death?"

VII

As MATT's BROW creased in amazement, Adam half-smiled. "Nobody talks about him, you know. He's sealed in a zone of silence. I've never known whether it was holy or accursed. I wish you'd tell me what he was like. You knew him better than anyone."

"Nobody knew him." Matt spoke with some vehemence. "That's what we found out and that's why we don't like to talk about him. Nobody likes to dwell on their mistakes. When I talk about Henry Villiers," Matt paused as Adam left the window and resumed his chair, "when I talk about him now, I wonder whether what I say means a damn thing.

26

He fooled us all."

He leaned back and an expression of perplexity crossed his face. "He floored us properly, your mother, Zoe, Wally and me.

"I thought I had his measure. We'd been friends since we were kids in the factory. We were both there because our dads said so, although he was headed for old Morgan's job and I wasn't looking much higher than five pound a week. I liked Henry, and I thought I had him sized up. I had him down as a first-rate craftsman. He had a good hand and eye, he could design and he could make. I felt he liked me. He talked to me sometimes about his plans, what he'd do when he was head of Villiers Glass. I understood he was quite happy to learn the ropes and sit in Morgan's chair one day. It wasn't a bad slice of life, after all. I thought, poor old Henry, he's not quite up to it but he'll scrape through. I patronised him. We all did. He didn't seem to resent it, he never complained, he never suggested he'd like to be shot of us. Just kept on as he was, mild and kind of reserved. Then one day when he couldn't stand us any longer, he walked out.

"Of course when he did that I started to think. I was pretty mad with him at first, you know. Angry because I'd backed him and he'd let me down. It was easy to fall into the habit of telling Henry what to do and like the rest of 'em I'd told away, told away. His parents told him to marry Grace, and he did. Grace told him to develop the safety-glass side, and he did. I told him to produce aircraft components, and he did. We were justified in our own conceit, we were building Henry up. After he walked out, I got to thinking; saw we'd been building ourselves up and shoving poor old Henry ahead of us like rubble on a snow-plough.

"We built him up too big. He'd have liked to be in charge of a smallish line, one factory at the most. He'd have enjoyed table glass, or making stage properties. Told me once he'd like to make a first class replica of the Crown Jewels. We had a good laugh about that, all of us, and made him President instead. It's a great game being a king-maker, Adam. Creating power is just as corrupting as taking power. Henry went on doing as he was bid, forming new departments, developing

27

new sites. I was up there with him all the while; the bright lad who'd learned the job from the bottom up. Wally was there to finance us and Grace was there to fire us with noble ambition. My God she was ambitious. There's something exhilarating about working with someone who's after the moon. She worked too, fifteen hours a day. She was clever, she had the seeing eye that can read events and see where they're leading.

"She warned us the war was coming. She'd travelled a lot in Germany, the Netherlands, Italy, France, and she used to hammer us to get ready for the war. That was back in 1934 when nobody wanted to know.

"Villiers was expanding fast by this time, and we were all working under pressure. It was about then that Henry's health began to fail. He'd always suffered from asthma, and in 1936 the attacks got worse and worse. We fetched him to all the best doctors, and they charged him top prices, but none of them told him to quit Villiers Glass, which was what he really needed to do.

"So one day he just started laying his own plans. He told me quite casually that he was initiating a new line, what he called facsimile jewellery. He was going to make glass copies of family heirlooms. It wasn't as silly as it sounds. In those days, people still owned wonderful jewels, and there were plenty of jewel-thieves working the smart areas. Rich folk used to put their real shiners in the bank and wear a good replica, which often cost several hundred pounds. Henry was all set to make these copies. He had everything worked out in his mind and he was as pleased as a kid that's found sixpence in the gutter.

"Middle of 1936 he went off to Amsterdam to sign on workmen. He came back with a crew of cutters and setters, among them a metal worker, name of Lisbet Jonkers. Henry gave them a place to work and started production. He took a surprising number of orders and he might have made a go of things, but you can imagine how we reacted. Here was Europe going into a war, big war contracts in the offing, and Henry wanted to make phoney diamonds. We had plenty to tell him about his duty to his country, and how he mustn't

28

tie up capital in childish ventures. There were some big shouting matches. At least, we all shouted. Henry just sat there quiet in his chair, polite as ever; looked out at the river and tried to breathe evenly.

"The winter of 1936 he had a terrible go of asthma. He went off to France to recuperate, and then across to North Africa. Later on, we found he'd taken Lisbet Jonkers with him. He came back home for Christmas and seemed quite happy. In fact he was happy, he'd found what he wanted and his mind was made up. In mid-January, 1937, he went home one Friday evening, packed one small suitcase, and moved into a room in Finchley Road with Lisbet. He left a letter for Grace, saying he didn't like his old life and was going to start another. He asked her to divorce him.

"Well, then the balloon was well and truly up. Conferences. Decisions. Ultimatums. Henry was to come home at once and behave himself. They picked me to carry that news to him. I went to the room; one double bed, bath under a plank in the kitchen. I took one look at Henry and realised it was no good talking. I told him I'd just come to see if there was anything I could do to help, and he gave me a smile and said, 'Yes, Matt, you can tell them to leave me in peace.' I went back to your mother and said Henry wasn't coming home.

"They didn't give up, of course. I tried to warn them, but they kept on at him. After a fortnight I went to see him again. I told him I was sorry I'd been a bloody fool all these years. We had a good talk. He told me quite calmly that he wouldn't make old bones, he'd spent most of his life trying to please us, we were damn difficult to please, and from now on he was going to please himself. What he wanted was quite simple. He wanted to get a divorce and marry Lisbet.

"That set me off again. I asked him whether it was wise for a middle-aged man in poor health to marry a girl half his age and from a very different background. He said he had no doubts about what he was doing. He was distressed about losing you, but he said that Grace had already shut him out of your life. He asked me to do what I could to smooth the path for him. I did. To my surprise, Grace agreed to divorce him, and he married Lisbet straight away and took her off to live in a house he'd bought in Norfolk. That was towards the middle of 1938.

"In name he was still president of Villiers Glass, but in practice he hardly ever came to London. We gave out that his health was bad. It was true enough.

"Each time I saw him, during those last months, he looked more ill and shrunken, but he was happy. Make no mistake, he was bird happy.

"As to Villiers, after Munich things looked promising. We'd been through a bad patch, the shares were low, but the Government contracts were coming in and we could see ourselves sailing towards the Happy Isles. By early 1939 we were up to our eyes in work, and we'd more or less forgotten about Henry.

"In May of 1939 he had a cerebral thrombosis. Grace, Zoe and I went up to Norfolk on the last day of May. When we got there we were told he was dying. He was almost totally paralysed and so was that silly wife of his. She simply went to pieces. Grace was very good, stayed in the house and looked after everything. Henry didn't know she was there, of course, but the girl seemed grateful. She spoke English badly and she relied on Grace to help her with doctors and medicines, and later on with the funeral. Henry died five days after we reached Norfolk. I came back to London to see to the work that was piling up, but Grace and Zoe stayed on to see him buried, and put the house with a good agent.

"By the time Grace came back to London, the Board had met. Kepple and I proposed Grace as President, and after a lot of argy-bargy that was accepted. In August 1939 she assumed office. She told me then she was acting regent for you, Adam. She's said so often enough since. It helped her at that time to have the responsibility. Helped her to get over Henry's death."

Matt fell silent, and Adam studying his face saw there the mark of old passions, old disappointments. He understood that without Matt his own childhood must have been deprived of male guidance, and he was touched by a deep feeling of reverence and love for the old man, so that for a moment he could not speak. At last he said, "Matt, I've never thanked you."

"Thank?" Matt's head jerked up. "No need, no need. And we've talked enough for one morning. I want to get out into my garden."

He pulled himself heavily to his feet and began to look about for the ancient jacket he wore out of doors. "And remember, Adam, there's no use worrying about last night. What will come, will come. We must just wait."

Adam, following him out into frosty sunlight, made a private decision to do what he could to shorten the waiting period.

VIII

ADAM RECOVERED THE card from Innes that afternoon, and took it back to Glass House. When he reached his apartment he saw that Grace and Zoe were basking in the thin sunlight of the patio.

Zoe was turning the pages of a trade journal, gesturing and chatting vociferously. Her meagre body was modish in a slacks-suit of orange velvet. Her kid-leather slippers, her lipstick, the vast rims of her sunglasses, provided the mandatory rose-pink clash. Her hair was arranged in curls that brushed her forehead. Yet as Adam approached he realised that her modishness was purely superficial. That boop-de-doop roll of the eye, that twittering voice, were no more than the stale smoke of the nineteen-thirties. They concealed a woman incapable of change and deeply hostile to all innovators. He understood for the first time that the greatest of all motivations in the acquisition and retention of power, is fear; and that all great enterprises must by definition include a certain number of frightened people.

Grace was stretched in a cane chair. A footrest supported her legs, a white mohair rug covered the lower half of her body. She wore a pale blue sweater with a silk scarf tucked in at the throat. She lay with eyes closed, pale and still as a patient under deep sedation. Only the fingers of her left hand moved, lightly stroking the arm of her chair, back and forth with a slow and searching rhythm.

As Adam's step reached the stone of the patio, both women turned to look at him.

"I've got the card." He held it up.

Grace extended her hand and he gave her the square of pasteboard. She glanced at it almost casually.

"The police were very quick."

"Not terribly interested."

Grace slightly lifted her chin, studied the card slantwise. "Amateurish," she said at last and passed the card to Zoe. "What do you make of it?"

Zoe held it between fastidious fingertips. "Tatty old thing, darling. It means nothing to me."

"No?" Grace's voice was calm and Zoe gave her a quick look. "I thought the writing was a bit like yours, when you do italics."

"Don't be daft." Zoe sat bolt upright. "It can't be. Wait, let's look." She bent over the card. A startled expression dawned. "Heavens, d'you know it might be? I did use that lettering many moons ago. Of course, so did almost every artist in the place, but I do admit it rings a little tiny bell." She giggled. "What a joke."

"Is it?" Grace spoke as if to herself.

"Well, rather like playing Planchette, don't you agree? Wherever did it come from? 'Happy Christmas, Henry darling.' I suppose I could have sketched it in the dim dark past. For a Christmas parcel, perhaps? Something like that?" Her eyes questioned Grace.

"Perhaps. When, though?"

"The good Lord knows."

"Think, Zoe."

"Lovey, how can I? Henry's been dead a good thirty years, you can't expect me to remember that far back, it isn't decent."

"It must have been before the divorce." Grace lifted herself higher in the chair and surveyed Zoe with the same quiet insistence. Zoe said nothing, and after a while Grace continued. "Before 1937. The Christmas of 1936 was the last one we all shared."

Zoe shook her head vaguely and Grace turned to Adam. "What did the police say about it?"

"That it's a type of card that's been produced in bulk for over seventy years. My prints are on it, and that soldier's. Innes held it by the edges. He says someone probably cleaned up the white spaces, fairly recently, with india rubber; and the chemists say it's been stored somewhere clean and dry, with camphor."

"With someone's private papers, I suppose, or in a store cupboard."

"Or office files," answered Adam. He turned back to Zoe who was sitting hunched forward like a bird. "Zoe, can't you remember anything more?"

"No. Honestly Adam my sweet, it's too long ago."

He was unsure whether to believe her. Grace had sunk back in her chair and closed her eyes. Their silence was a gently-closing door. Adam put the card in his pocket and went back into his flat.

IX

THE NEXT COMMUNICATION was a letter, delivered by hand.

The clerk who received it was a punctilious man, and instead of placing it in the chute for the Mail Department, he summoned a messenger and had the letter taken to Adam's secretary on the Board Room floor.

To his surprise, that brought Adam down in person. He came hurrying across the foyer to the Enquiries Desk, the letter in one hand, the envelope in the other.

"Ted, did you take delivery of this?"

"Yes, Mr. Villiers. Seeing it was marked Urgent and Personal, I thought it best to send it right up."

"Yes, thank you. It's unsigned. Can you remember the bearer?"

"Yes, sir. It was a young woman. I remember her quite clearly. She was about twenty-eight, I'd say. Not a kid, but young-looking. Dark hair, and a kind of strange face, a strong face if you know what I mean? Not the usual type of girl.

33

Quite a full mouth and rather a short nose but with sort of thin nostrils. Very dark eyes. She had a scowling way at first, but when I'd taken the letter she suddenly laughed, quite gaily you know? Her teeth were very good, you don't often see such white teeth these days."

"You're observant, Ted."

"Well, I am, sir, it helps in my job to remember and take note. But . . ." Ted hesitated, searching his mind, "I noticed her specially, because she was so . . . she had such a head of steam on, know what I mean? Kind of concentrated energy? And she looked as if she'd seen a lot of the world and wouldn't give you much for it. She wasn't at all an ordinary sort of girl."

"Did she look sound in the head?"

"Sound? Oh yes, I mean I didn't say much to her, but she certainly looked as if she knew what she was about, very buttoned-up, I'd say, sir."

"What was her voice like?"

"That was the other thing. She never said a word. Just handed me the letter, watching me, frowning. Pointed out the urgent and personal notice with her finger. I called the messenger and gave him the letter. I asked if she'd wait for an answer and she shook her head. As the messenger went away she suddenly laughed. Then she gave me a funny, mocking sort of bow, and out she walked."

"How was she dressed?"

"She had on a white coat, one of those synthetic furs. Quite bulky. No hat. I didn't see her shoes."

"Thanks, Ted, you've been most helpful. If you don't mind, I'd like you to keep quiet about this."

"I'll do that, Mr. Villiers. And notify you if she's here again?"

"Please."

Adam returned to his office, closed the door against the gaze of his secretary, and spread the letter flat on his blotter. There were two sheets, good vellum paper. The first bore no address of any kind, and was undated. It ran:

"Dear Mr. Villiers,
Your father collected jewellery, perhaps you do too. Anyway, you're rich enough, aren't you, now that you're going to be President? I thought you might like to buy a certain piece at present in my possession. I enclose a description of it. If you want to know more, write to Mr. Eugène Thiers. He knows me. He can set a fair price on it. I'd like to discuss price with you, though. Maybe we can meet some time and talk about that.

Yours very truly,
Emma Salt."

Adam laid the first sheet aside and turned to the second. After studying it briefly, he pressed a button on the intercom set and said, "Miss Fergusson."

"Sir?"

Adam hesitated. Jessie Fergusson had been Grace's personal secretary for fifteen years, knew everything about Villiers Glass, was discretion itself, yet Adam found himself unwilling to confide in her now. He said, "Will you please check with Credit Bureau and also with Personnel and Overseas, to see if they've got anything on a M. Eugène Thiers, of 57 Rue Montluçon, Paris 7e? He's probably a jeweller or connected with the trade in some way. Get me anything you can on him, as quickly as possible."

"Certainly. Mr. Villiers, you have an appointment with Mr. Grant-Rice at ten."

"Oh blast. Yes, all right, thanks Jessie."

He switched off the intercom and went back to his scrutiny of the second sheet. This was slightly larger than the first. It bore the letter-head of Eugène Thiers et Cie. The design was modern, lower cap lettering, a lot of white space. The text below was in English, typed, and brief.

TO WHOM IT MAY CONCERN.

This is to certify that I have examined the sunburst brooch in the possession of Miss Emma Salt, the description of which is as follows:

"Ten-branch sunburst of late eighteenth or early nine-

35

teenth century design. Framework of gold filigree wire on plain gold base. Central boss decorated with single dark red cornelian, and round it alternate brilliants and seed pearls. This boss can be made to revolve by a clock device."

The design and workmanship of the brooch are good. The stones are small but of fair quality. In my estimate, the insurance value of the brooch is £275. There may be added values for the curiosity buyer, but this aspect needs fuller investigation. A detailed valuation can be supplied on request.

December 11th, 1967.   Eugène Thiers.

Adam rubbed a hand across his chin. He had small doubt that the Emma Salt of this correspondence was the woman he had seen approaching Glass House on Christmas Night.

The threat implicit in that first approach was reinforced by the tone of her letter. Blackmail seemed the obvious explanation. Yet surely a blackmailer did not indulge in a malicious joke, and the next week deliver a letter in person to the victim and take good care that the reception clerk remembered her?

The letter from M. Thiers set the face value of the brooch at £275, not a great sum. Emma Salt's letter spoke of wealth, the need to discuss price. That implied blackmail, yet again there was something off-beat about the threat, a derisive note.

Ted had said she gave him "a mocking bow". Mockery had been the disquieting element on Christmas Night.

Derision and determination, these seemed to be the characteristics of Emma Salt's actions.

Well.

Adam folded the two sheets of paper and tucked them into his breast pocket. He went from his own office to the Export Department to keep his appointment with Mr. Grant-Rice, who appeared to know everything about metallography, and almost nothing about the cost of manufacturing bullet-proof glass.

When Adam returned to his room some time later, Miss Fergusson handed him a memo from Frost of the Overseas Agents Department.

Re: M. EUGÈNE THIERS.

M. Thiers is a jeweller of note, specialising in the manufacture of modern jewellery for the very rich. He has a large exclusive clientèle in Britain and America. He has occasionally corresponded with us about maximum-safety display-cases. He is said to be eccentric, but is of high repute among members of his trade. Has a large private fortune, including considerable holdings in the Amsterdam diamond market.

It seemed unlikely that such a man would conspire with the unknown Emma Salt to threaten, defraud, or even mildly annoy a respectable firm of British glass merchants.

Nevertheless, Eugène Thiers provided a link with the woman. One would have to write to him.

As he reached this conclusion, Adam realised that already he had begun to dance to Emma Salt's tune.

X

ON THE NIGHT of December 27th, Grace went down with a feverish attack. Her doctor, a needle-eye named Fraser, was called in and examined her. When the examination was over, he spoke to Adam in Grace's dressing-room.

"I don't think there is any infection. We have to remember that she's getting by on one kidney and that's not in good condition. She tells me that two nights ago she went outside in evening clothes and stood about in the cold. Now that's just madness, Adam. She must not put such strain on her body. And she must avoid worry. She's got something on her mind, I can see. She won't discuss it with me. Do you know what's bothering her?"

"Perhaps. Someone played a rather unkind practical joke on us, on Christmas night. It was just a hoax, but it distressed her."

"Naturally. What a lot of unpleasant people live in this world, eh? Well, I shall send you something to steady her down. She must stick to her usual regimen, keep warm, rest, and not worry."

"One of her worries is whether she'll be fit to travel to Norfolk for New Year."

"I know. Why she chooses to go there in winter beats me, but I know it's important to her, so we'll have to try and get her well enough for the journey. I've told her I'll call in to-morrow morning, we'll see how she is then."

When Adam entered Grace's bedroom, he found her propped up on half a dozen pillows, a writing-case on her knee. He went over and took the case away from her, placing it on a table some way from the bed.

"Dr. Fraser says you're to rest."

"Just thank-you letters." The delicate lines of her face were blurred and puffy. Her skin had a brownish tinge.

"Those can wait. If you want to go to Norfolk, you must do what your doctor tells you. And stop worrying."

"Not very easy, is it?"

"That card troubles you?"

She hesitated a moment, as if between two lines of thought. Her eyes, the beautiful grey eyes that illness could not dim, gazed at him uncertainly. Then she said, "Naturally, it troubles me. Someone has been cruel enough to taunt me about my husband's death, and at Christmas time. It was meant to make me unhappy, and it has."

"In point of fact the card was addressed to me. And why does it cause you unhappiness? Shock I can understand, distaste; but unhappiness?"

"You don't understand." Her head rolled impatiently. "Henry's death was a great grief to me. Time doesn't alter that."

"When he died, you'd already been divorced for over a year."

"What has that to do with it?"

"Well, surely, you divorced him? Your feelings can't have been so intense? And after thirty years . . ."

"You know nothing about it. A marriage is not to be judged piecemeal, not on one event. Not on one year. Henry and I had a good marriage, we were perfectly happy until that last absurd incident."

Her voice was calm, her expression bland. Adam was silenced for a moment. Then he leaned forward and tapped the thick silk of the counterpane.

"Now look. You divorced my father on the grounds of his adultery with Lisbet Jonkers. After the divorce he married her. You can hardly describe that sequence of events as an incident, absurd or otherwise."

"But I can, Adam, and I do."

"Are you trying to tell me that my father was satisfied with your life together? Was he happy in his marriage, in his work, what did he want out of life, what made him turn to this girl? Things like that don't just happen out of the blue."

"But they do. Life is full of ridiculous events. Human beings are often stupid and impulsive, that is one of the things one learns. I'm afraid, Adam, that you've been talking to Matt. Matt has a blind spot about Henry. He always blamed himself for the way Henry let the Company down, so he's always tried to find excuses for Henry. I believe it makes Matt feel good to think he 'gave Henry a year of happiness'. It's very annoying for me. Henry wasn't unhappy with me. He was an intelligent, sensitive human being, and he was complex in everything he did. He loved experiments. Lisbet Jonkers was one of them. If he had lived, he'd have acknowledged a failure. That is all. That final phase of his life has no real significance, you know. Lisbet Jonkers was a breeze on the surface, she was much too slight to reach the depths of Henry's heart and mind.

"Henry was a deeply religious man. He was not brought up to countenance divorce. He could not have looked on a wedding in a registry office as anything but a sop to the law. There was never the slightest doubt in my mind that he would realise his mistake and return to me. I knew that the only way to keep him, was to release him for a space. He had to find out the truth for himself. And the truth, Adam, was that your father and I were married. We were tied together by God, by common work, by common interests, by our child. These are lasting things. And so I told Henry when he asked me for a divorce. I was right. Time has proved me right. Lisbet is

39

gone. And here I am, here you are, owners of Glass House, running the Villiers Glass Company, spending our New Year in Norfolk just as we have always done. Everything is exactly as it was."

"Except, my dear, that my father isn't with us."

"If he had lived he would be here with us tonight."

"You can't know that."

"I do know it."

"Don't you think he would have built a happy life with Lisbet?"

"No. They simply weren't suited. From her point of view, I assure you, his death came at exactly the right moment. Six months of marriage, then he died, before he was disillusioned enough to set her aside. She was lucky in that, although later the luck turned against her, poor creature."

Grace settled back against her pillows with the air of having said all that was necessary. Adam found her calm deeply disturbing. He had long known that in the business sense she had blind spots. She took a line and held to it with incorrigible conviction. Part of the present weakness of Villiers Glass stemmed from that rigidity of mind. What he had not fully realised was how far this trait permeated her entire life. Clearly she had never accepted the divorce from his father. Over the years she must slowly have buried the true facts under a cocoon of illusion.

It followed that the events of Christmas Night were a very real threat not only to some nebulous and forgotten past, but to the whole fabric of her present. Grace must not be told about Emma Salt's letters. If possible, the whole nonsense must be resolved without involving her further.

Aloud, he said, "Tell me what happened to Lisbet after my father died. Matt said you helped her."

"Yes. I felt I must. She was quite helpless. After the funeral I stayed to sort out Henry's clothes, arrange about the lease of the house. I had to explain the terms of the will to Lisbet and see she took what she wanted in the way of furniture and household effects. She had no idea how to behave, no experience of money."

"Did she inherit much?"

"Yes. She received her due share of Henry's estate. We settled things amicably and quickly. None of us wanted the affair to drag on; even the lawyers made haste. The war was coming, you see? Lisbet's one idea was to scurry back to Holland. She was Dutch and her family was there. We all tried to make her see that she was crazy to go back, but she was stubborn as well as stupid. We settled accounts here and I took her back to Amsterdam. I found her a nice little apartment, and saw her settled into it. She had plenty of good furniture that Henry left, and silver and glass: everything she needed to make her comfortable. That was in July 1939. When the war broke out, I tried to get her back to England, but she refused to come. Perhaps she'd already made contact with her Nazi friends and felt safe. In May 1940, when Holland was invaded, we lost trace of her altogether."

"And after the war, did you hear from her?"

"Not from her, but of her. She'd become a great collaborator, you see. It didn't do her much good. She got through all the money Henry left her, sold up all his furniture and other things, and some time in 1943 she died, in a hospital for poor people. Pneumonia after measles. I'm afraid I've always felt it was exactly the way one would expect Lisbet to die, of some rather footling disease. Still, one couldn't help pitying her. She must have been very lonely at the end, without family or friends.

"Perhaps it's as well she died when she did. After the war, I applied to various organisations who were busy tracing lost people, and I found out that she was on the blacklists as a collabo. Some of her countrymen might have given her a rough time had she lived."

Grace sighed and shook her head. "It all seems so long ago, and so . . . unimportant. What matters is the present, us, our work. Adam, I'm so glad that we've had this little talk. It's brought Henry closer to us both. He'd be so proud to see you President of the Company.

"And I want to tell you that I have the utmost confidence in you, the utmost confidence, my dear. You've got difficulties to meet but I know you can carry this job. You have a clear head, and you have my ambition and my feeling for administration, but you have something of Henry in you too; something of his reserve and constraint, which is all to the good. I want you to do well, but more than that I want you to enjoy your Presidency. I enjoyed mine. It's a wonderful experience to head a great enterprise."

"I'm sure it is."

"You don't sound very convinced."

"I'm convinced." He smiled at her. "I like my life. I like being rich and free to put big plans into effect. I'm a commercial animal by breeding and training."

"Are you?" Grace put out a hand and touched his face. "Sometimes I feel that you're quite detached about the Company. Not emotionally involved at all."

"I take the view that life is a good deal more than just Villiers Glass."

"Well, of course one must lead a full life, have outside interests."

Adam was silent. That very phrase, "outside interests", proclaimed the gulf between them. Never in a thousand years could he explain to her that life, for him, was not an area with fixed boundaries, but a flood into which one plunged; that the constant change, the struggle to keep head above water, was what one sought, not what one avoided.

He said gravely, "I shall try to confine life to its proper place, which is outside business hours."

She smiled up at him as he rose to his feet. "Are you going out tonight?"

"Yes, taking Kate to the airport."

"Where's she off to?"

"Ireland."

"She's charming." Grace watched him. "Could it be special?"

"Could be." He bent and kissed her. "You do what the doctor orders. Rest."

"Shall I see you tomorrow morning?"

"I don't think so. I think I may go over to Paris. I want to follow up Zoe's visit."

Grace was at once diverted. "Yes. Try and find out why

Zimmerman wouldn't take Jet Set. I expect Zoe bungled it. She's made far too many mistakes lately. It really is time she retired."

XI

M. EUGÈNE THIERS was tall, spindly, about fifty-five, with inquisitive eyes and a pursy mouth. The tip of his long nose was blunt, as if he'd stuck it once too often into someone else's business. He was impeccably dressed, insulated against the icy wind that rasped the face of Paris. An old-fashioned felt hat perched at a challenging angle on his head, a fine cashmere scarf was folded decorously between the lapels of his excellent overcoat. His English was perfect and he talked without cease in a high and honking voice as they forged their way through side streets and across minute quadrangles.

"A taxi is no use here, as you see. We shall soon arrive and be in the warmth once more."

"I do apologise," said Adam for the tenth time. "Dragging you from home at this time of year."

"No, no. I'm delighted. I find holidays so boring. I am not religious, Christmas is not a festival for me, in fact I'm waiting only for my wife to resolve some family problems, then we are off to Chamonix. I have a chalet there you know."

"You ski?"

"Yes, extremely well. And you?"

"Extremely well for an Englishman."

"You should come and try our French resorts."

"Perhaps I will."

They marched through gates into an ancient yard, entered a small and surprisingly elegant building and juddered heavenwards in a lift that had apparently been designed by Ronald Searle. M. Thiers, leading the way into an office on the third floor, explained that this was not the main branch of his business. "There one has the sort of edifice the public expects, a great deal of wall and floor and the

43

most modern fittings. I find it very unsympathetic to my nature. It contains the vaults for our stones, and armchairs for our impossible clients. I keep this little place here for my own use. I can be quiet here and think, I can arrange useful discussions with patrons who do not wish to advertise their dealings with me. In case," he waved Adam across a snug and thickly-furnished drawing-room to a small study, "you imagine that I conduct nefarious trade with dishonest clients, I beg you at once to rid yourself of the notion."

"What sort of people do come here?" Adam snatched at the line thrown him.

"Royalty," said M. Thiers firmly. "Buyers of rare stones and antique jewellery. People who wish to sell valuable pieces without starting a rumour that they are bankrupt. And a few interesting people, like your Miss Emma Salt."

"She's not mine."

"Truly? She seemed to know so much about you. Do please sit down."

Adam settled himself in a leather-covered chair and accepted a glass of very good sherry. "What did you think of her?"

"Secretive. That was my immediate impression. Such a flat eye, such a long quiet mouth, one finds in a woman who knows secrets and guards them with care. I am going to tell you about her, Mr. Villiers, because quite simply that is what she wishes me to do."

"She said so?"

"She came to me; asked me to set a value on the brooch, and write a statement. She said to me, 'When Mr. Villiers gets in touch with you, answer any questions he asks.' You notice she said, 'when', not 'if'."

"That doesn't sound secretive."

"Not at first. Thinking it over after she had gone, I decided she had told me only what she wanted to tell. She said nothing of her reasons, nothing that revealed herself. It was a business deal for which she paid without question, and I assure you my price is high."

"Isn't it unusual for you to see such a client personally?"

"Most. I was fascinated, you understand, by something . . .

quaint . . . in the tone of her first letter. She wrote to me at this address, in itself not a common line of approach. She must have made certain enquiries. Her letter I thought very clever. It did not precisely threaten, it was not precisely arrogant, but there was something inexorable about it. It reminded me quite of my priest when he talks about the building fund. She made it clear that since I was going to see her some time, it might as well be at once. That impressed me. Also I was interested in her description of the brooch. I made an appointment with her and she came here on December 10th."

"Can you describe her to me?"

"Yes." M. Thiers did so, giving a description that tallied with that of Ted, in Glass House. However, M. Thiers knew more about clothes than Ted ever would. "I noticed her coat, particularly. It was so out of character with the rest. She wore, you see, very good things. Her shoes I judged to be Italian, hand-made. Her dress was of very soft wool, probably with a mohair mixture, and although it was not by a great house, it was good enough. She had a handbag of excellent quality and design. I study such details because I match the jewellery I make to the personality, and the clothes are indicative. I thought to myself that day, 'Here is a woman well-dressed, well-arranged in every respect, yet over the top of that dress she puts a coat of the most revolting aspect; white nylon fur, vast and ill-cut. It made her look like a home-made teddy-bear.' Now why?"

"To attract attention? Everyone who has seen her mentions that coat."

"Ah? That would certainly uphold my impression, namely that Miss Salt wishes to make contact with you. She knows that, like many wealthy men, you are not easily approached. She devises a way that will catch your interest. She executes a careful plan with determination and skill. One must almost admire this young woman, she's original."

"Indeed."

"Of course," Mr. Thier's nose suddenly expressed wistful sadness, "I shall never know the outcome of the story."

"I'll tell you about it, if I can."

"Will you? I confess to a formidable interest. Also, I'm concerned from the professional viewpoint. That brooch Miss Salt showed me was not in the ordinary run of things. I think at this point you must examine the papers."

He went away, to return in a few minutes with a cardboard file, balanced on top of a large book with a blue suède cover.

He handed the file to Adam, who glanced through it. As M. Thiers said, Emma Salt's letters were strange; they gripped, and they menaced. At the end of the collected papers were a copy of M. Thier's detailed valuation, and of his letter to Adam. Behind the last, lay a coloured photograph, and a scale drawing showing the structure of the brooch. Adam frowned at the photograph for some time, then looked up.

"Haven't I seen it somewhere before?"

For answer, M. Thiers picked up the blue book and spread it on his knees, leafing over the pages with quick, delicate movements. When he found the place he wanted, he swivelled the book round to face his guest.

Displayed on the page in wonderfully clear detail was a picture of the brooch, the same as the one in the colour photograph in Adam's hand. He leaned forward and held the photo beside the picture. There was no question. They were identical, the same ten spiky branches of filigree gold, the same red stone at the centre, with surrounding brilliants and pearls. He glanced at M. Thiers and found that sharp-shooter unashamedly gloating.

"Yes. Identical at first glance, Mr. Villiers. Yet this . . ." he tapped the page . . . "is a little toy created some 175 years ago, for the Empress of Russia's great friend, the Countess Kostroma. The central boss is a single ruby. When that is made to spin by the little clock mechanism, the stone refracts light. The effect is of a living flame, bizarre of course, the joke of a very rich woman. Nevertheless, the sunburst has historic value, and intrinsic value. It is worth . . . several thousands of pounds . . . if it still exists."

"Why do you say that?"

"The Kostroma sunburst has been missing since 1939. At that time it was in the possession of the Paris branch of the Kostroma family. When the Germans invaded France, the head of the family tried to send certain valuables to Switzerland. Jewellery, plate and several paintings were sent off in a truck, but they never reached Basle. Somewhere between Paris and the border the truck vanished. Since the war one minor picture has been recovered, but none of the jewellery has ever been traced. I imagine the settings were broken up at once, and the stones dispersed or re-cut."

"Do you think Miss Salt planned to cheat you by passing off the fake as the original?"

"No. She made no such attempt, in fact she told me at once hers was not the original brooch. It was this frankness that I found so intriguing, Mr. Villiers. Why did she come to me, since she did not wish to sell me the brooch? Why did she explain that she was going to send my valuation to you? Why did she instruct me to answer your questions? You see, she invites curiosity. Almost, she insists that I wonder why the Kostroma is of interest to you."

Adam met the merchant's probing eye. "I can guess why she came to you. She wanted the opinion of a man whose skill and integrity are beyond question."

"Thank you, monsieur."

"As to the rest, I'm floored. Do you think the present head of the Kostroma clan could tell us anything about the fake brooch?"

"Sad to say, no. To confess, I have made discreet enquiries. But the main line of the family was eliminated by the war, and the present holder of the title can't help at all. He was in Poland most of his life, and hardly knew his Paris relations. There are no written records of what happened in 1939. One must infer that the copy was made at the request of the Kostroma of that time, but one cannot prove it."

"One other thing, M. Thiers. Can you describe Miss Salt's voice?"

"That is not easy for me. English is not my home language, I find accents hard to place. Her voice was quite low, but resonant and expressive. I noticed the vowel sounds. The 'a' was a little shortened, and I thought she might perhaps be American. Then I thought not. The accent was not strong, you understand; more a hint, a shadow of something learned as a child."

"Could it have been Australian? They flatten the 'a'."

M. Thiers shrugged. "I would have recognised that, I think."

"New Zealand?"

"Perhaps. I can't be sure. It seems to me, thinking back, that this woman may have been to all these places. She had the air of one who has travelled. More than that, of a woman who is . . . without fixed abode? Is that the right phrase?"

"Yes. A displaced person."

"That is so. And Mr. Villiers," the merchant leaned forward and the light from the window showed a disquieting glint in his eyes, "I do not need to warn you that such a person, without a fixed abode, without any allegiance, can be the most dangerous of all the untamed beasts."

XII

"Adam! When did you get back?"

"An hour ago. May I come in?"

"Of course, sweetie, you must be frozen. Have you had dinner?"

"I had something on the plane."

Adam followed Zoe across the hall and down the flight of honey-coloured marble steps that led to her living-room. This was warmed to steam point. Indeed, the decor of the apartment, recently altered by Emelia Hornbeck, gave an effect of chronic over-heating. There was too much florid pink and antique gold. One felt that somewhere in this juicy pomegranate lay a bruise that might darken overnight into decay.

Walter Kepple was already present. He was stretched full-length on a circular couch, apparently dozing, a book on his chest. He wore an expression of complacency, as if he were thinking, "All this is very expensive and quite amusing, but it is expendable. I, on the other hand, am unique and cannot be duplicated even by God, who is after all the finest

48

of all artists."

He opened his eyes as Adam approached, and was instantly wide awake and smiling.

"Aha. Welcome home. Why are you staring at me in that fierce way?"

"I was thinking you look damn pleased with yourself." Kepple, whose ability to read people's thoughts was sometimes frightening, watched Adam with a sardonic air. "It must be this room. Brings out the worst in me. So, did you sell Jet Set to old Zimmerman?"

"I didn't try."

"And welcome truth, though late it comes. Why?"

"Why should he?" Zoe's tone was sullen. "Zimmerman wouldn't take it from me, why should he take it from Adam?"

Adam pulled off his overcoat and dropped it across a chair. "Is that coffee hot?"

"Certainly." She poured a cup and brought it over to him. There was an uncertainty in her movements. The small lines that creased her upper lip were stained with lipstick; a piece of swansdown clung to the thin curls at her temple. Adam reached up and removed it. "Jet Set doesn't matter that much. There's something more important. I've asked Matt to come round. I'll tell you the whole when he's here, if you don't mind waiting."

Kepple sat up on the couch and slid his feet neatly to the ground. His regard was round and blue as a Persian cat's. "One small thing. Who did you see in Paris?"

"A jewel merchant called Eugène Thiers. Here, read these." Adam took from his pocket Emma Salt's letter and Thiers' guarantee, and handed both to Zoe. She glanced at them, shook her head and passed them on to Wally. He took longer over them, turning the pages in his small strong fingers. Giving them back to Adam, he said, "Why didn't you mention these earlier?"

"There wasn't time. I wanted to get over to France at once."

A faint smile touched Wally's mouth. "You have hidden depths, haven't you, Adam?"

"What do you make of the woman's letter?"

Kepple shrugged. "You seem to have become the target for the malice of a crackpot."

"What do you think she wants?"

"Money," said Wally without hesitation, "and maybe notoriety. The thing has the stink of greed."

"Yes, I agree."

They fell silent, waiting for Matt to arrive. Wally picked up his book of poems and riffled the pages. Zoe wandered about the room, her arms wrapped across her chest, her feet in their gold mules scuffing peevishly as a child's. Adam sat thinking about what Kepple had said.

Wally was wise in matters of finance; he also knew something about greed. But there were greeds other than avarice. What did Emma Salt want? Mr. Thiers said she was not poor. Did she want to be still richer? Was she after higher stakes than the £275 quoted as the basic value of the brooch?

Wally had said Adam was the target. Was this so? Could Miss Salt be aiming not at, but past him; at someone who stood close to him?

And why did one take her seriously? Why not dismiss her as one dismissed other cranks, turn the letter over to the legal department and forget it?

Too close to home? Too near the bone of truth?

The woman had gleaned a surprising amount of information about Villiers Glass, its personnel; about the late Henry Villiers. She'd managed to lay hands on that card, perhaps by theft or trickery; might have bought it, might have been given it. The giver could only be someone long in the service of the Company—or high in its ranks.

At eight-twenty Matt arrived. He rolled down the steps, greeted the company, and lowered himself into a chair. Adam gave him the letters and he read them carefully. When he was done, he pinned them under a massive elbow and said, "I take it you saw this chap Thiers today?"

"Yes."

"Let's have it, then. Zoe, for God's sake sit down and keep still."

"I'm worried, Matt."

"It won't help to squirm about like a worm in a bloody

apple. Well, Adam?"

Adam described as concisely as he could the meeting with the jeweller. At the end Matt said, "And what does Mr. Thiers think about it?"

"He got the impression Miss Salt is out to attract our attention."

"Well, so she has done, hasn't she?"

"And that," said Wally, "I find very interesting." He ran a finger down the spine of the book he still held. "Why do we bother our head with the creature? I suggest we hand the whole thing over to the police. If Grace boggles at the idea of a public turn-up, then we can hire a private eye. We've done so before."

Zoe interrupted sharply, "Don't be a fool, Wally."

Kepple said mildly, "I am merely asking . . . "

. . . "You are asking for some detective person to come nosing into our affairs, that's what. We'd have no secrets left, it would all be too sordid and miserable."

"Anyone would think you had a guilty secret, Zoe dear. Why should we fear an investigation?"

"I certainly don't plan to discuss my private life with some total stranger, and nor does Grace, let me tell you."

"I think we can leave Grace out of this."

"Oh, don't be so pompous. How the hell can anyone discuss your private life and leave out Grace?"

The words, flung out in fury, produced a moment of complete silence. Matt glanced swiftly at Adam and saw bleak withdrawal in his eyes. Zoe, having said the unsayable, pouted, shrugged and proceeded to make matters worse. "It's no good mincing matters. Grace told me last night she wouldn't have the police prying about. A private eye would be just as embarrassing. We must face facts."

Kepple said, "When you interrupted me, I was about to express my surprise at the effect Miss Salt has had on us. All of us, I don't exclude myself. Certainly she has tried to create an atmosphere of malice and suspicion. What puzzles me is how well she's succeeded. We're all rather more upset than the surface situation warrants. I think we must find out why this is so. There's more than a hint of blackmail in the woman's letter. A blackmailer, may I remind you Zoe, bases his trade on the possession of unpleasant facts. Miss Salt evidently possesses facts. I suggest we try to emulate her. I want to know more, much more, about Miss Salt. By all means let's face facts, but to face them we must first possess them. For that reason I suggest a private investigation. It may be unpleasant, but I believe it's necessary."

He glanced at Adam who was sitting quietly, his gaze fixed on the glowing base of the lamp beside him. As Adam made no move to answer, Matt intervened.

"Have you thought that the woman may want us to make enquiries? She's probably a crank, after publicity. Isn't she trying to force us to take action? I just don't see her as a blackmailer. She's never tried to hide her identity, for one thing, she went to see Thiers as calm as you please. She doesn't seem to fear the police at all, which means she's got no police record."

"She may be a psychopath," pointed out Kepple, "anxious to give us as much trouble and pain as she can. A psychopath can be careless of consequences. She may have a record as long as your arm."

"Thiers didn't seem to think she was psychopathic. In my view, she's a crackpot, a show-off, and I don't think we should play her game for her. I say, sit tight and say naught, and let the lady come to you. What do you say, Adam?"

Adam stirred in his chair. "I thought of Philip Boyle. He fixed the thefts at the Derby works, he knows us fairly well and he knows how to keep his mouth shut. I agree with Wally. If Miss Salt is a crank, then we must put a stop to her nonsense. If she's a blackmailer, then it follows she's found out something she thinks she can use against one of us. If we knew what it was, we might be able to deal with it ourselves and tell the woman to go to hell." He put out a finger and slowly traced the outline of the lamp's base.

"If you're suggesting we confess our sins," said Kepple with some bitterness, "I'm afraid I have nothing to offer that isn't already public property."

Matt said heavily, "There's no need for us to start suspecting one another. It's not only sinners who are open to blackmail. Most of us would put down good money to protect someone we're fond of, and blackmailers know it. If we just keep quiet and bide our time the problem will settle itself."

"I don't think we'll be allowed to keep quiet," said Adam. "It's too late for silence."

"What do you mean?"

"Emma Salt already has some lead into Glass House; a man or woman we know well."

"I don't see that."

"Look, Matt. Somehow or other she has managed to get hold of a Christmas card that Zoe drew and autographed for my father. An item like that could only come from his private records. Those are stored in the vaults in Glass House, and the only people who have access to them are the four of us here, and of course my mother. So the question is, by what means did Emma Salt obtain that card?"

Zoe said petulantly, "I didn't know a damn thing about it. I can't remember drawing it, it may not even be my writing. All italic script looks the same."

"An easy statement to make," said Kepple, and she rounded on him. "You shut your teeth, you jumped-up little clerk. I don't need your bloody insults."

"Long ago, Zoe, when you were a girl, rudeness was fashionable, but fashions change."

"Then don't call me a liar, that's all." She turned to Adam. "I expect the Salt creature stole the card, or perhaps she got it from someone we don't even know. After all, it could have been lying about any old where, all these years, in some old book, or at the back of a cupboard. There's nothing to show it came from Glass House."

"Yes, there is, quite a small thing." Adam put his hand in his pocket and produced the card, turned it towards them. "This number in the corner, one-eight-three. My father used to number his records like that."

"So what?"

"One doesn't number a Christmas card, so it looks as if this is part of some collection, or index." Adam glanced casually from one face to another, and found each wary,

53

brooding. Kepple spoke first.

"Very well, let's take the positive line that the card came from the Villiers papers in the vaults. In which case Miss Salt could have obtained it only through one of us. To begin with, the vaults are locked and only we have access."

"Cartwright has a key."

"To the outer vaults, yes, but not to the saferoom. That's got a combination lock. What's more, we have keys to turn off the burglar alarm system, but Cartwright doesn't. Henry's records are all in the inner safe, and therefore accessible only to us four here, and Grace. That seems to exonerate Cartwright." He touched an eyebrow with a delicate finger. "I rather think the first confession must come from me; just to start the ball rolling, you know. On Christmas Night, when I left Grace's flat at midnight, I went down to the vaults. It occurred to my nasty suspicious nature that it could do no harm to check up on Cartwright's checking-up. I found the vaults undisturbed, and the burglar alarms set. When I reached the inner safe, however, I saw that some-one had been before me. There was a handsome seal on the door, impressed with your signet mark, Matt."

Matt nodded. "Yes. I went down to the vaults on my way out of the building. That would have been about eleven-thirty. As Wally says, everything seemed to be in order. I opened the safe-room, and went in. The shelves were tidy, the filing cabinets were locked. I don't think anything had been moved recently. Things were a little dusty."

"That doesn't mean much," said Adam. "The card could have been taken months ago. We've been in Glass House over two years."

Kepple's eyes shifted from one to another. His smile was wafer-thin. "All these precautions, Matt, and you said nothing to a soul? And Adam, nipping over to Paris with-out a word to his co-directors?"

"I told my mother I was going."

"But you didn't tell me. No, I'm afraid all this confirms my opinion that we need to put a few cards on the table. It may not disclose what's in Miss Salt's hand, but at least it might reveal what we hold ourselves, don't you agree?

54

I suggest we call in a private investigator tomorrow morning."
Zoe made a sound of protest and Matt said quietly,
"Adam, let it rest."

But it was to Kepple that Adam spoke.

"I'll let you know tomorrow morning what I have decided."

XIII

UPSTAIRS GRACE VILLIERS lay in the bed that her husband
Henry had designed for her at a time when only a thin
line divided the luxurious from the ludicrous. Posts of
Venetian glass, pale gold, supported a blue silk canopy
embroidered with cherubs and flowers. Silken curtains were
looped back to the posts. Over the blankets billowed a
coverlet of white swansdown; as if beneath some springtime
sky, drifts of snow still lingered.

Grace was quiet, remote. It seemed that all this splendour
hardly concerned her. The lamplight shone on the high
curve of her forehead, on the pallid knuckles of the hand
that held a fold of the sheet under her chin.

The telephone at her bedside rang, and without opening
her eyes she stretched out her left hand and lifted the
receiver slowly to her ear.

"Yes?"

"Grace, it's Zoe. I have to talk to you."

"Talk then."

"In private."

"No-one is listening." The woman in the bed scarcely
seemed to be listening herself. Her face was sealed in intro-
spection.

"That card. Adam's suspicious. He knows it's part of a
set."

"There is no set."

"You destroyed them?"

"On Christmas night."

"Oh, thank God."

"It makes very little difference." Grace opened her eyes.
"I checked through them before I destroyed them. Several

were missing, enough to prove that they formed a sequence. And don't forget that each card can be tested against the original."

"Who could have known they were in your apartment?"

"Anyone who has been close to me in the two years I've lived here."

"But you don't let just anyone into your apartment, Grace. You certainly don't even let friends go to your cupboards."

"They were in the camphor-chest."

"Well, who goes rumpling about in other people's store-chests? And why would anyone steal the card, anyway? I don't understand it. I'm frightened."

"There is no need to be frightened, yet."

"The servants? Could it be one of them?"

"It's extremely unlikely, isn't it?"

"Someone might have bribed them? I mean, if it's not them, then it's one of us, and it can't be."

"There may be another explanation."

"Adam thinks it's one of us. So does Matt. Adam's going to call in a private detective. I tried to stop him, but he won't listen to me. He won't even listen to Matt. Grace, what can we do?"

"Be quiet, Zoe. Stop whining and listen to me. You must keep your head. No crime has been committed, remember that. There has been no crime. No one can harm you, not even the police. All we need to do is keep calm and wait. The past is finished and dead, stone dead, it can't touch us."

"Yes, it can. It can. It's come alive again, it's . . ."

"Goodnight, Zoe."

Grace pressed the receiver gently back on its cradle. She reached under the pillows and drew out a clean handkerchief and passed it slowly over her brow and upper lip.

The room with its rich contours, its exuberant soft colours, was inappropriate to her. It was too frivolous to match the austerity of her illness. Sometimes she longed for a bedroom in a mountain clinic, where she could lie in a cot between plain walls and see, through the window, a white uninterrupted slope, a section of barren sky. In such a setting one might be able to combat pain with dignity.

After a while, she turned her head slightly, so that she could watch the french doors to the terrace on her right. In time she heard the expected footsteps, advancing up the flagged path, crossing the lawn, running up the stone stairway. Knuckles brushed the glass of the door. She put out a hand and pressed a switch on a panel beside her. The lock released, Kepple swung the door open and stepped across the room to the foot of her bed.

"Well, my dear love? How are you?"

"Better tonight. I'll be up tomorrow."

"We'll see." Kepple leaned forward and studied her with concern. "You're in pain? Have you been getting out of bed?"

"No." She smiled faintly. "It's gone. Tell me the news, Wally."

He shifted sideways a little, one hand touching the dressing-gown thrown across the foot of the bed. "Adam called us together tonight. He thinks that card was stolen from Henry's personal records. Can you throw any light on that?"

"Not a ray." Her face expressed a gentle astonishment, and Kepple's gaze became derisive. He moved round and perched on the end of the bed, put out a hand and grasped the ridge of coverlet and blanket over her toes. Half mocking and half sad he said, "You can trust me you know," and he gave her foot a little shake.

She made no answer, and he shrugged. "Well, I don't think it came from the vaults. If you think of any other solutions, let me know."

She nodded. "I promise."

"Your promises!"

She smiled sleepily and he smiled back, the hand still gently moving her toes back and forth. "One more question. There was a nurse who looked after you last year, for a few days. Remember?"

"Vaguely."

"Got a picture of her?"

"Gracious, no."

He sat quietly watching her, and as no interest showed in her face, he said, "All right, forget it." He got to his feet and Grace spoke quickly, "Wally, I'd answer your questions if I could."

"Of course." He bent forward and brushed the back of his hand down her cheek. "Shall I stay a while?"

"No. I'd rather be on my own."

Kepple knew that she had a strange attitude to illness, she preferred to fight it alone, she seemed to draw strength from solitude. His anxious gaze could not discern any sign of pain or fever now, though, and he hesitated.

"Sure there's nothing I can fetch you?"

She shook her head. Her eyes closed. He leaned and kissed her lightly.

"Sleep well, then, my darling."

She did not watch him leave. He put out the lights, went through the door. She heard him tug it shut, and the lock click home. She listened as his steps retreated across the terrace.

When she was sure he was out of hearing, out of sight, she switched on her bedside lamp, and climbed slowly out of bed. She crossed to the dressing-table at the far end of the room. She opened the top-right-hand drawer, took out an address book and carried it back to bed. She sat hunched against the pillows, shivering a little, and turned the pages of the book until she found what she wanted.

XIV

On December 29th, Wally and Matt Kinsman drove to Sussex to inspect a factory-site on which building had just begun. They finished their work by noon, and on the return journey stopped for lunch at a pub on the banks of the Arun. The country was still deadlocked by cold, the ditches frozen, the reeds by the river immobile and crystalline; as stiff, thought Matt, as Wally Kepple, and he knew that this resentment must be breached at once.

Over steak and a bottle of Chambertin he made his plea. "Wally, I'm sorry about that seal. I just wanted to keep things quiet and not worry Grace. I'm sure Adam feels the same. That's why he said nothing to us about the Paris trip. There was no intention of keeping you in the dark, nothing like that."

Kepple sipped his wine. "I accept that. What does rather stick in my gullet is that you appear to believe one of us is guilty of theft."

"Eh? Oh, come on, I never suggested that."

"You implied it, Matt, when you put the seal on the door. Nobody has a key to the inner saferoom except us. Therefore you sealed it against us."

"I didn't think it through. I just . . ."

"I have thought it through. I've reached a certain conclusion. None of us is a thief. None of us broke into the safe. The card was stolen by an outsider, and from some point outside the firm's vaults."

"Meaning?"

"That the set or index series containing the card was removed from the safe some time ago and taken upstairs."

"By Grace?"

"Obviously."

"Why would she want index cards?"

"Simply because they carried Henry's handwriting. She keeps all his clothes still. All his books and pictures are upstairs in that library, and she's often said she should have all his letters, even the business ones. She hoards anything that provides a link with him. It's an obsession."

Kepple's voice was trembling, his face suffused with colour, and Matt suddenly felt deeply sorry for him. He said, "An obsession, maybe, but that's not devotion, Wally. She's made a sort of cult of Henry because he slashed her pride to ribbons. She's spent years wiping out every trace of the divorce. She wants the world to forget it ever happened, and she's damn near succeeded. Most people think of her as Henry's widow. It's crazy, but that's how it is."

"If she's stopped loving Henry, why won't she marry me? I've asked her often enough. She's ill, she's tired, she's not young, we're well suited. Darn it, Matt, I'm sick of being Kepple the backstairs man, the boy on the make. I'd marry her now if she'd have me, but she won't. And time's precious. I may not have her for long. I just want to look after her.

That's all I ask. Can't she let me love her? Can't she trust me for that?"

There were actually tears in Kepple's eyes. Matt knew that only a truthful answer could ease his distress. "The fact is, Wally, Grace doesn't trust anybody. She knows that if she married you, she'd lose the whip hand over the Company. She wants Adam to run Villiers Glass, not you."

"You think I'm chasing Grace to get my hands on the till, is that what you're saying?"

"Not me. Some say it."

"More fool they." Kepple gave a sudden wry smile. "If I didn't love Grace, I could take the Company. When you go, in a year or two, I could take it. I've backed Adam to please Grace. She knows that."

"And she also knows you're an ambitious bastard who doesn't like playing second fiddle. Be honest with yourself, Wally. Would you take orders from Grace if you were married to her? She'd lose her grip on Villiers. With Adam as President, she'll retain it."

"You think we're a lot of pirates."

"Ay, the lot of us. We'd none of us be where we are now if we hadn't known how to look after Number One. Grace knows you, and she knows herself, so she won't marry you. She's a realist."

Kepple stared at the plate of food before him and suddenly thrust it aside. "She's not realistic about Henry."

"True again. And that's what worries me. This Salt woman seems to know how Grace feels about Henry. Otherwise why did she plant that card? I wish I knew what it all meant. If we knew why it scared Grace and Zoe, we might be able to stop the nonsense at once. I've been wondering, did Zoe do the drawing as well as the writing? She swears she can't remember, but true and false don't signify with our Zoe."

Kepple's lashes flickered. Watching him, Matt saw his mouth curl with a secret glee. Wally had clearly remembered something, and whatever it was, he wasn't going to tell. That was the trouble with Wally. You felt sorry for him, you stuck your neck out and confided in him, and next moment he was doubling back on you, ready to pull some stunt of his own.

60

He'd been born to outsmart everyone, himself included. Matt let the subject drop; but back in London he sought out Adam in his office, and told him of the conversation. "Wally's on to something and he's going to use it without consulting us. I know that look of old."

"Well, I set him a precedent."

"Bull. You kept a close mouth because you didn't want to worry Grace. So did I. With Wally it's different. He's going to do himself a bit of good at someone else's expense. Could be yours. He's no friend to you, Adam. Don't give him any chances."

"I won't." Adam's voice held a certain grim amusement. "He may give me one or two. If he does, I'll take them."

"Good. But don't throw him too hard. We need him." Matt smiled, but his eyes were tired. "And watch your back."

Adam reached into the top drawer of his desk and pulled out a folder. "I telephoned Phillip Boyle this morning and asked him to come round. We had a talk. I told him we're being nuisanced by a woman who may be a crank or a blackmailer. He's agreed to make enquiries for us. I know you aren't happy with that, but. . . ."

"I've changed my mind. If you don't call in Boyle, Wally will get someone else without asking us. And if there's going to be dirt shovelled, I'd rather hold the shovel myself. Did Boyle have any ideas?"

"He asked to see my mother." Adam opened the folder and took out a printed form. "She showed us this."

Matt's eyebrows lifted. "Of course, that's it. Is Boyle following it up?"

"Yes," said Adam. "He started this morning."

XV

PHILLIP BOYLE WAS good at his job. On graduating as a chemist from London University, he had spent several years at a research laboratory in Leeds. Later he came south again, became interested in forensic science, and was for a time attached to the London C.I.D. When he quit to start his own private detective agency, his colleagues were astonished.

They were even more astonished at the success he made of it.

It took time, of course, but within ten years he headed a staff of competent men and women. He was able to choose his cases and refuse all divorce work. His income impressed the accountants who looked after his books, and he had a healthy and growing list of private investments. His pleasant flat in a quiet district south of Gloucester Road was furnished in a way that bespoke taste and money. He had a really excellent collection of porcelain. Astonishing, his friends said; but Phillip Boyle was in some ways an astonishing man.

He was nothing to look at. A bland oval face, long hazel eyes, a plump, quiet mouth. His physique was neither soft nor hard, his voice neither loud nor soft, he had a sidelong glance neither challenging nor humble. He seemed the sort of man one wouldn't notice, and yet people noticed and remembered him.

He was held to be a man without passions, yet he had them. A passion for porcelain figures, which cost money and demanded a good deal of care and study. A passion for observation, for looking and remembering, for filing away at the back of the mind. A strange, intense and disciplined passion for disentangling the skeins of a man's life.

Boyle did not claim to understand human beings, nor did he particularly like them. He observed them. At times, when he was paid to do so, or when he felt so inclined, he would stretch out his plump yet delicate hands, lay hold of a life, disembowel it and spread out the separate strands for examination. He made no attempt to explain the dissected parts. He certainly could not weave them together again in a healthier or more beautiful form. There was nothing of the philosopher or healer in his make-up. As a peasant accepts the fact of migration without understanding it, so Boyle accepted the eccentricities, perversions, and criminal habits of the human race.

He was not dishonest. He had standards to which he adhered fairly strictly. And though he lacked the warm qualities that make a creature lovable, he did possess considerable physical courage.

Above all, he was inquisitive, and he had the inquisitive person's instinct for a secret.

It was his curiosity that made him take up the Villiers case, as much as the substantial fee offered. It was his experience that made him decide to work on it himself, and to use an unorthodox approach. It was his lack of physical fear that prompted him, when he found himself being trailed, to continue on foot and along the darkest alleys.

He had supped, as he often did, at an Italian restaurant in Earls Court Road; and after he had shared coffee and a chat with the owner, he left and started to walk home.

It was about eight-fifteen, and there were plenty of people on the pavements, plenty of vehicles on the roads. It was not until he turned off along the back streets that led to his flat that Boyle realised he was being followed.

The tracker was using a car. In his experience, two sorts of people did that; the amateur, and the professional thug who valued speed above anonymity. Both categories could prove dangerous, and Boyle's first instinct was to cut across the blocks by footpath and lose his company. But curiosity got the better of him. He could not, thinking quickly, guess at any client or subject who would be likely to chase him in an Austin Cooper. The car was noisy, to say the least. Unless the person wished to be noticed?

The idea came unbidden, and Boyle examined it as he walked. Almost automatically, he went through the routine of testing his follower. He put on speed, slowed and doubled. The car kept track. Finally, smiling gently, he walked round all four sides of a square. The Austin followed at a circumspect distance, but with no attempt at concealment.

Standing on the corner, Boyle studied it. Green and white, newish. He noted the number, but could not distinguish the occupant's features. He continued on his way.

A nut? Something different, anyway.

Boyle's apartment was in a converted Victorian house at the end of a cul-de-sac. There was room for a car to turn there, but no parking-space. He reached the building, climbed the front steps, took out his key and fitted it into the lock, opened the door a fraction. He could move inside fast if he had to, but he didn't feel it would be necessary.

The little car turned into the cul-de-sac and came towards him. It turned and slowed, stopped directly opposite where he stood. The window rolled down and a woman leaned out.

She wore a thick white furry coat, and her dark hair hung loose on her shoulders. She was dark-eyed, and her skin was deeply tanned. The fog-lamp directly above her threw greenish shadows under her cheekbones and beneath the full lower lip. She studied Boyle calmly, turned her head and appraised the house behind him. She looked back at him and smiled. Her hand moved. She wound up the window, revved the engine, and drove off along the alley.

Boyle wrote the registration number of the car in his notebook and went into the house.

Upstairs, he went straight into the living-room. It was a large room, painted white. A number of modern cabinets lined the wall opposite the three long windows. Boyle's collection of porcelain was housed here. He drew the curtains, snapped on the heater, flicked the switch that illuminated the cabinets. He chose a chair close to the case of Chinese Red, and sat down to think.

So that was Emma Salt. For some reason she'd chosen to follow him home, had made sure he saw and recognised her. Well, that tallied with what he'd learned earlier in the day. Adam Villiers had said she was careless of recognition. Seemed almost to have a craving for it.

A loony, or a smart girl? One thing was certain, she was getting a big kick out of this. Sitting there in the car with a look-at-me-Charlie smile.

So perhaps she meant to show him she knew all about him. That could be. Might have been tipped off by someone in the Villiers household. Servant or someone.

Might have . . . Boyle wriggled in his chair as a far more disquieting thought struck him . . . might have known all along they'd call him in.

That was more like it. She was a cool one. She'd collected a pile of info about them, knew all their past history; probably had a pretty shrewd idea which way they'd jump. She must have known for sure they'd check up on her job, go to the bureau and ask questions. And you could bet she had some friend there who'd tell her who came asking questions, and what those questions were.

Nerve. She had plenty of nerve and more. When she knew they were after her, she didn't make a run for it, not at all, she came driving round in an Austin Cooper, grinning all over her face. Mad.

Mad, or smart. A smart player, and impatient. Needling her opponents, as good as saying, "Speed it up, your move and be quick about it."

Boyle's nose twitched. Interesting. He stretched out a hand to the telephone, then remembered that Adam Villiers was not at home. Addressing the Lucas Group on automation as a means to productivity. Boyle's neat mind ticked off the fact.

If Adam was out, then who? Matthew Kinsman was probably in church, bellowing his head off in some Christmas Cantata. Kepple it must be.

Boyle dialled Kepple's number and was answered almost at once. He reported the incident of the Austin Cooper. Before he reached the end, Kepple interrupted him. "Could you identify the driver?"

"I'm coming to that, Mr. Kepple. It was Emma Salt."

"How can you be sure?" Kepple's voice was so rancorous that Boyle was taken aback.

"I can be sure. I have positive . . ."

"All right, not on the 'phone. I'm coming round to you. What's your address?"

Boyle gave it; and as he hung up, he wondered what could be bugging the Big Money man.

While he waited for Kepple to arrive, he went into the kitchen and took beer from the refrigerator. He also cut a plate of chicken sandwiches. Although he avoided heavy meals, he was a constant nibbler. He liked things nicely served, and spent some time arranging the sandwiches on a cut-glass dish, with chopped lettuce and stuffed olives and thin slivers of cheese.

He carried the tray of beer and food back to the living-

65

room, set it on a table close to the heater, crossed to the centre window and watched for Kepple's approach.

A few minutes later Kepple came into sight at the head of the cul-de-sac. He was on foot, and wore a dark overcoat, the collar turned up. He hesitated a moment and then came forward. His rapid gait expressed anger and something else, excitement perhaps. As he drew near to the house, Boyle pressed the button that unlocked the front door.

Kepple's step came up the stair. Boyle opened the door of the apartment and Kepple thrust forward, into the light, turned and stood with shoulders hunched, eyes glittering.

"Now, Mr. Boyle, will you kindly tell me how you're so sure that the woman you saw tonight was Emma Salt?"

XVI

Boyle faced his guest with a stolid look. "By her photograph, Mr. Kepple."

"What photograph?"

"The one the nursing agency gave me."

There was a short silence. Kepple turned abruptly away and moved towards the far end of the room. His mouth, Boyle saw, was compressed in a tight and humourless smile.

"Would you like a drink, Mr. Kepple?"

"No thanks. All right, yes, yes I will." Kepple bent over the tray, jerked the cap off a bottle of beer and tipped it into a glass. He sat down in the nearest chair, hooked one arm over the back and said, "give me the details, please."

"Certainly." Boyle poured his own drink, handed the plate of sandwiches to Kepple, who waved it away impatiently. "This morning, Mr. Villiers asked me to call round at his office. He explained the situation regarding Miss Salt, and asked me to conduct an investigation. Naturally, the first thing I wanted to know was whether she'd had any previous contact with Glass House, particularly with the senior personnel there. I asked Mr. Villiers to let me talk to his mother. She told me that last year, she employed a private nurse for some days. Mr. Villiers did not remember the woman, as he was away in Scotland at that time; but Mrs. Villiers looked up the name of the agency that supplied her."

"I see." Kepple was staring at the amber liquid in his glass as if he saw the future there. "Aren't we a tricky bunch, to be sure? Oddly enough, I'd thought of that nurse. I planned to tip you the wink about her, but it seems I was slow off the mark." He rose and wandered over to the middle of the cabinets against the wall. "A fine collection you have here. I'd like to own that plate. So you checked with the agency?"

"Yes, at once. I know the proprietress, as a matter of fact."

"And she gave you a photograph of Miss Salt?"

"An impressograph copy of a photo. The woman was not registered with them as Salt, but as Van Staden."

"Yes, I recall the name now. The identification is beyond doubt?"

"Yes. The picture tallies with the description given by the clerk at Glass House, and with the appearance of the woman who followed me tonight."

"Can I see the photo?" As Boyle minutely hesitated, Kepple's brows rose. "Mr. Boyle, you called me, I didn't call you. If you've changed your mind, say so and I'll go home. It is possible, however, that I can identify the picture. I saw that nurse."

"Of course." Boyle pulled the photograph from his pocket and handed it across. Kepple studied it closely.

"That's her. Looks a bit cheerier than I remembered. She struck me as being a sullen piece."

"Perhaps she didn't like you."

"Perhaps." Kepple continued to scan the picture, and at last said musingly, "not unattractive, feature by feature. Rather striking, in fact. Is she still on the agency's books?"

"Yes, but she hasn't worked for them recently. She first registered with them two years ago. She had references from two of the best doctors in New York, and one from Dr. Kevin Fraser who happens to be Mrs. Grace Villiers' doctor. She worked on several cases for Dr. Fraser after she joined the agency. Said she liked working for one doctor, turned down most of the other cases offered to her. It seems she's a very good nurse, with a great deal of experience with rich elderly patients. When Mrs. Villiers asked for a special for a few days, through Dr. Fraser, it seemed natural to send Nurse Van Staden along."

"You think that's what she was aiming for?"

"It seems extraordinary, but true. We'll have to try and find out how she crossed Dr. Fraser's path. If she deliberately ingratiated herself with him, knowing him to be Mrs. Villiers' doctor, then she's incredibly patient and persistent."

"What's her financial position?"

"My information from the agency is that she has a private income. She gives or gave no impression of needing to earn her living. Told them she loved nursing and wanted to keep her hand in. She was so damn efficient they jumped at her whenever they could get her. She's a dab at handling rich old bastards that no-one else can cope with."

"Van Staden. Are you checking her New York references?"

"Yes. I've got Runyan's checking on her time there. But there are plenty of Dutch names in New England and New York. Tracing her may take time."

"Plenty of Dutch names everywhere," said Kepple. He reached out and collected a sandwich, bit into it with sudden relish. "Mr. Thiers of Paris said she spoke with a faint accent. He seemed to think it might come from Australasia. The Dutch East Indies is probably thick with Van Stadens. But," he swallowed and dusted crumbs from his fingers, "the place where there are the most Dutch names is still Holland. That, you may remember, is the place where Henry Villiers' second wife was born and died. I think you should visit Holland."

"Mr. Adam Villiers thinks so too, sir."

"Indeed? Good for him. Foresight and resource, our Adam shows. I seem to have underestimated him."

"It's easy, with those quiet ones. He's no fool." Boyle's long eyes regarded Kepple sleepily, and after a moment the latter glanced casually back at the cabinets of porcelain.

"Sotheby's exhibited some delightful white last month. Did you buy anything?"

"Beyond my touch, and outside my period."

"It was certainly very pricey." Kepple's chin dropped on his chest. He took a pace towards the window, turned.

"How long will you be in Holland?"

"I'm not sure. A few days, perhaps a week. I don't think I'll get much."

"You're going to make enquiries about Lisbet Villiers, I take it?"

"It seems a possible lead."

"Interesting. Fascinating." Kepple lifted his head and looked straight at Boyle. "I should so much like to hear about it. I suppose you'll report to Adam at the earliest possible moment?"

"Of course."

"Ah, then, I'll hear all about it . . . in time." Kepple's smile was blinding. "Thank you for your report about the car, I'll tell Adam of it tonight, if he's home early enough. Otherwise, first thing tomorrow."

"Thank you."

Kepple moved to the door. Reaching it, he paused for one last gaze at the cabinets. "An expensive hobby," he said thoughtfully. "If ever you have a little spare cash, and want a useful investment, let me know. I may be able to put you on to something good."

"Kind of you, Mr. Kepple. I'll remember."

"Not at all. One good turn deserves another."

Kepple was gone.

Boyle walked to the left-hand cabinet. He opened the door with a key taken from his pocket, lifted out a small vase and turned it slowly in his hands. His mouth pursed and straightened and pursed again.

Kepple was prepared to put down cash, nice and tactful, in exchange for private info about the Holland enquiries.

Boyle set the piece back on its shelf.

Mr. Kepple should know that reputable agencies did not break confidence with the man who paid the bill.

That, at the moment, was Mr. Adam Villiers.

On the other hand, behind Mr. Villiers stood a very powerful company. Who had the final word there? Kepple was the Finance boss, but just how far did he control the others?

Boyle sighed.

He'd have to take his orders from Adam, but treat the rest

of 'em with the utmost care.

He picked up the photograph of Emma Salt otherwise known as Emma Van Staden; and stared at it for some time before putting it away in his pocket.

Someone in Glass House knew what that face signified. Perhaps all of them knew. But no-one was telling.

And after all, thought Boyle, if clients told all they knew, then there'd be small room in the world for private investigators.

XVII

WHEN ADAM AND Matt left London for Norfolk on December 30th, the afternoon sun was already rolling in the dun light like a turnip in a stew. Grace, Zoe and Wally had left the city earlier, and Adam drove Matt's big Mercedes since the old man disliked driving in the dusk. They spoke little until they were clear of the urban fringes, but as they reached Cambridgeshire, Matt heaved himself up in his seat and said, "I suppose we can thank the Salt woman that you're with us for New Year?"

Adam made no reply, and Matt said, "How long since that last happened?"

"About six years, I suppose."

"Well, you have your own friends."

Adam's thin profile, that so closely resembled his mother's, turned a little away from Matt. "I'm not bound to the old patterns."

"No. That's right. But you can't sweep everything aside at once, you know. Even in Glass House, you can't do that. And up here. . . ." Matt paused, and Adam took the chance to alter the sharp angle of the conversation.

"I shall make some changes."

"Such as?"

"Spend less on packaging and P.R., more on distribution, computerisation, and market research." Adam swung the car north at an intersection. "And Design's a mess. I'd like Koch to take over control there when Zoe goes."

"Has she talked of going?"

"She's not up to it, Matt. Wally agrees with me."

"And your mother?"

"Zoe's blackmailed her long enough." The word struck an odd note, and Adam's hands shifted uneasily on the wheel. He accelerated up a long straight incline, and as they topped it said impatiently, "This weight of tradition is dangerous, Matt. Half the time it means you're doing something for no intrinsic reason. So much tradition is hailed as necessity. You see it in the churches, the government, business, half our institutions haven't much relation to reality. It's not a matter of age, of course, there are plenty of customs five thousand years old that still make sense because they express present needs in the most effective way. But there are rules only a year old that are hopelessly outdated. One of the problems in industry is to strike a balance between continuity and redundancy. What I'm trying to say is, I won't make changes just for the sake of it, I'm not that sort of new broom, but I do intend to look at things carefully and chuck them out if they belong on the village dump." He edged past a labouring tractor, saluting the driver with his left hand. "This annual trip to Norfolk, for instance, I don't understand why you put up with it. None of you likes sailing, or shooting, none of you wants to sit in the marsh and watch birds or anything. So why in God's name spend New Year in a grotty cottage? It's not my cuppa."

"We are escaping from it all." Matt's mouth turned down in a sardonic grin.

"You? You love London."

"Grace needs solitude."

"No she doesn't. She needs all of you."

"Umh. Umh." Matt's smile faded, and he said more quietly, "She goes to visit your father's shrine. She makes the pilgrimage and we carry the baggage."

"My father," said Adam carefully, "lived there for a few months. God knows why."

"It has a sort of beauty. Sea, hills, the marsh if you like mud. Henry did."

"A helluva place to bring a new young wife."

"Ah, now there you're wrong. Lisbet liked Norfolk. She really liked it. She came from that sort of place, herself. Kept a picture on her dresser in the kitchen, her Ma and Pa and four other kids, all standing beside a boat, with dykes or polders or whatever you call them behind. Your father bought her a boat, and she sailed it often. She liked birds, too. Come to think of it, she was a sort of goose-girl type. Long straight hair, and a bit adenoidal. Dimmish. But pretty."

"How come a goose-girl spent her last years in Amsterdam?"

"They often do. You ought to read your folk-tales again. But she was city-trained, after all. A metal-worker. Perhaps her friends were there."

Adam shook his head. "No friends. She died alone. A goose-girl? That's not what my mother says. Your picture might be truer than hers. Has it struck you, Matt, that what's happening is that while we watch, the scenery's changing? I mean, we're getting a new slant on things, on the past? A silly goose-girl you say. My mother says, a silly schemer. Which?"

"Silly, that's certain."

"Yet my father married her. Did he like silly women?"

"Your father could be damn silly himself, at times." Matt gave a half-chuckle. "Yet I don't know. I'm beginning to think he proved us wrong. In the 'thirties, the war was coming up like a locust to the young leaf. We were dead keen on industrial expansion. Wally and I scrounged capital, boy we bled for it. Meantime, Henry prattled about coloured table glass and costume jewellery. He said that's what people would be after, when we'd won the war. We said, if we win it. In 1938, when we were really sweating on the top line about Hitler, Henry was planning a world where every woman wanted a red glass dinner-set. Another thing he was designing was plain decanters with shallow engraving on the front face only. We had a good laugh about that, Zoe and I. But when the war ended, what did people want? Red glass dinner-sets, and plain decanters with shallow engraving. For years the Scandinavians and Italians wiped the floor with us. So you see, Henry was a fool in the short term, but not in the long. Maybe it was the same about Lisbet."

"You think the marriage might have worked out?"

72

"God knows. Maybe. If he'd lived long enough." Matt fell silent, and after a while said, "When he died, I should have stayed in Norfolk and seen to things myself. I shouldn't have left Grace up there with Lisbet. It's easy to see things after the event, or as you say, in the light of new events."

The Mercedes swept north, skirted Ely and crossed into Norfolk. The villages with their fine tall churches showed the flint and thatch of that country. After Downham Market the terrain became more rolling, the cold of the land was veined with the cold of water, and the moon lumbered up lop-eared and glaring in a frost-blue sky.

After a time they could hear and smell the sea. In a last fold of dry land they found the farmhouse. Beyond it stretched the long dunes, pierced by creeks flooded now with the full tide.

As Adam stopped the car they heard high above them the rataplan of wings, and saw a solitary wild bird swing in to settle on the marsh-land to the west.

Matt climbed out stiffly and gazed about him. He stood so for a moment, then turned to Adam.

"I could have stopped Grace buying the farm, for one thing."

"Not if she'd set her heart on it."

"She hadn't. She didn't want the house for itself. She bought it to exorcise Lisbet, and she's failed. Every time I come here, I know one thing. This place belongs to Henry and Lisbet. You know it, don't you? We all do, except Grace. Wally's tried time and again to make her sell it, Zoe hates the sight of it. When I'm here, I know that Grace is living a dream. She's closed her eyes to Lisbet, but Lisbet took Henry. Lisbet won."

"She also died."

"Did she?" Matt turned his head away and muttered, "Death shall have no dominion."

"You're letting your imagination run away with you."

"Hmh!"

"Tell me something. Remembering Lisbet, do you see her as a thief?"

Matt took his time answering, then said, "I don't think so.

She was grasping, she was stupid, but somehow I don't think she was a thief. And your father certainly wasn't. Look, I've said some rough things about your father, lately, but understand, he was a man people loved. He was . . . he had a lovable personality, that's all. And he was honest. Not just surface honest, but right through. That's something I like to remember about him. It's a part of something I love, see? I don't want Henry's memory mucked about. And if I feel like that, how does Grace feel? If anyone starts a scandal about Henry, what will it do to her? Adam, I think she'll go mad."

"Emma Salt will name her price, in time."

"Yes." Matt glanced once more at the desolate stretches of sea and land. "But God knows if we'll be able to pay it, in blood or money."

XVIII

THE HOUSE HENRY VILLIERS had bought for his bride was some hundred and fifty years old, an unpretentious farmhouse built to withstand extremes of weather. Over the past quarter of a century, Grace had modified its structure; included an immense window in the living-room that faced the dunes and the sea; made over the kitchen and added two bedrooms and a bathroom on the lee side of the building.

There was ample hot water, adequate cupboard space, oil-heating. Most of the rooms had a good fireplace, and fires burned throughout the cold spells, driftwood sometimes, or more often timber from the fruit orchards to the south.

Yet the house was not touched by these improvements. It was like some patient animal, tricked out in finery by children, yet retaining its own character, biding its time against release.

Even the servants, a woman called Mrs. Jervey and her daughter Amelia, a handyman and gardener named Swinburn, were alien to the London party; people from another world, they might have felt sympathy for Henry and his goose-girl, but they clearly felt none for Grace and her friends.

This antagonism of place and people had not in the past affected them as sharply as it did now. It seemed to Adam that each of them felt acutely vulnerable here, all the urban defences lacking, the mind somehow exposed to primitive emotions in this primitive setting.

He felt too the presence of Emma Salt. Although she was not discussed, she encroached upon their thoughts; she seemed to have moved physically closer. Her voice murmured in the incoming tide, and the cloud shadows that stole colour from the landscape were also the shadow of Emma Salt.

Zoe was worst affected by the solitude. She wandered restlessly about the house and garden. Her manner became more and more disturbed, she was drinking too much. On the afternoon of New Year's Eve, she was missing from the group round the fire, and Grace sent Adam in search of her. He found her on the terrace that overlooked the sea.

It was four o'clock, and the light was going. A cherry-red bloom shone on the thin wash that lapped the high-water mark. As Adam came up to where Zoe stood, she turned to him with a scowl.

"What do you want?"

"Mother wondered where you were."

Zoe stared out at the sea, her shoulders hunched. "I don't need company."

"Is there anything I can do?"

"You?" She broke out laughing, and then said in a rapid mutter, "why should I discuss anything with you, you tell us nothing."

"What do you want to know?"

"Boyle. He's gone to Holland, Wally says. Why?"

Adam watched her closely. "To see the Amsterdam police, among other things."

Her head jerked round. "What a fool you are, Adam. Do you think that's not been tried?"

He said abruptly, "Zoe, do you remember the Kostroma robbery?"

She gave an impatient shrug. Her attention seemed to be wandering. She fixed her eyes on the seaward view and mumbled again, "Go away, leave me alone."

"What do you expect to see out here?"

Her hands beat a tattoo on the rail. "She's close. She's somewhere close, I can feel it."

"Who? Lisbet's ghost? Come inside, Zoe, you'll catch your death of cold."

She leaned back, straightening her arms. "Ah, but it's colder in there, with my friends. They freeze me. Darling Wally and dear old Matt, and you, Adam. Our new president, our new cold little animal of a president who sees everything and says nothing."

"You're rather drunk." As Adam spoke, the suspicion and dislike that had festered between them for years suddenly flared and she swung round with a snarl.

"My God, I wish I were drunker. Then I wouldn't have to look at you, I wouldn't have to talk to you. You think I don't see what you're up to? You want to get me out. Don't you?" She raised an unsteady hand at him. "Don't think I'm blind. You won't shift me. It's my life. My department. We built it up, Grace and I. I knew her before you were born, before Henry, before anyone. I know everything she is and everything she's done. You won't shift me. I'm here to stay."

He gazed at her with anger and revulsion. She was a limpet, a simple sucking organism, incredibly tenacious. He said, "No-one is trying to get rid of you."

"Don't lie." She spoke with such fierce contempt that he checked; and as he looked down at her face, he recognised the justice of her accusation. He had slipped deeper than he realised into the pattern of deception they all wove. Was there indeed an independent Adam Villiers, who could make a free decision or an honest statement? As he groped for an answer that would satisfy himself as much as Zoe, she pulled away from him and moved along the terrace, her arm raised.

"There! She's there!"

Adam spun round. Zoe took another stumbling step. "Up on the ridge, above the creek!"

"There's no-one." Yet as he spoke a figure came into sight, hurrying down the dunes with a springing stride, the head uplifted. Adam laughed. "It's only the boy from Oatham, with the papers."

Zoe shook her head. She covered her face with her hands and stood trembling. Adam moved towards her.

76

"Zoe? I'm sorry if I've been unkind. Can't you tell me the truth? I could help if I knew what was troubling you. Is it something that happened here? When my father died?"

She glanced up at him almost without recognition, as if her thoughts were on something a long way away. Then she turned and with the same uncertain gait, made for the house.

Adam let her go. He felt oddly detached from his environment and the people within the building. Was it true, what Zoe had said? A cold animal at heart?

The terrace was almost dark. He stood waiting for the boy to come up to him, took the newspapers, proffered a couple of coins.

"Tell me, did you see anyone on the dunes?"

"Yes sir, a young leddy." The boy was backing away, eager to be off.

"Thanks. Happy New Year to you."

"Happy New Year." Already the voice was fading in the wintry air.

Adam's eyes searched the dim line of the coast. Was she there? He felt again the strange pull of her. She drew him from the light and warmth, from friends and certainty. In her ambit, the line of his purpose seemed to waver, his very identity seemed in doubt.

He found himself leaning forward, almost ready to scramble up the dunes and seek there some sign of her presence, some footprint that might be hers.

It was with a conscious effort that he turned his back on the shore, made his way into the house and closed the door.

XIX

"I SAW HER. She was up on the dunes, staring down. When I moved, she disappeared."

"Adam thinks it was the newspaper-boy you saw."

"Adam had his back to her. Matt, you only believe what you want to believe. She's here."

"Well," Matt pressed tobacco into a leather pouch with deliberate fingers, "if she wants to play bog-bogles, that's her business. Can't harm us."

"Aren't you going to look for her?"

"No. That'd be just what she wants, no doubt."

"You're a fool."

"Maybe. My conscience is clear, though. Can you say the same?"

"You mind your own business."

"I intend to."

"I did see her, Grace."

"It's possible."

"It's true."

"All right, I believe you."

"Wally believes me. He's going to look for her, he's going to check all the pubs and hotels round here until he finds her."

"And then?"

"Well, at least he can confront her."

"With what?" Grace stretched out a hand and took a cigarette from the packet beside her. "Can't you understand, Zoe, that we can't stop Emma Salt at this stage? Later there will be a way to deal with her."

"Perhaps Wally already knows one."

"If you're hoping that Wally will knock the creature over the head, you can rule that out. A woman clever enough to steal the card is certainly clever enough to leave a signed deposition with someone, to be opened in the event of her death." Grace described a delicate circle with the hand that held the cigarette, watching the smoke riffle and drift. "No, Zoe. She has certain information. She will do the confronting. She at the moment directs the pace, and it pleases her to make us suffer. But sooner or later the confrontation will come, and we will break her."

"What if she breaks us? Adam asked me if I remembered the Kostroma robbery."

"Whatever has that to do with us? If he wants to chase up blind alleys, let him."

"I have a presentiment of evil."

"What you have, my dear, is a skinful of whisky. I advise you to cut your liquor consumption, get plenty of sleep, and keep calm."

"Calm, my God!"

"Calm. I have told you over and over again that the worst that can happen is a certain amount of unpleasant talk. Whatever Miss Salt knows, she can't damage us materially. We are within the law, we always have been. You must remember that, and you must stop indulging this hysteric mood. As for Wally, let him chase about the countryside. It keeps him occupied, and it might even prove useful. If he finds the woman, he'll come and tell me."

"He may not. He's absolutely furious with you because you didn't tell him about that nursing agency, and then the next minute you go and tell Boyle and Adam."

"I told them because Wally was already on the scent. It looked better to give the information voluntarily, don't you agree? As to Wally, I can manage him, don't worry." Grace patted Zoe's wrist. "So cheer up, darling. You can rely on me, as I rely on you. Now be an angel and fetch the cards. We'll have a round or two of Samba, shall we, before dinner?"

At the door, Zoe turned. "Even if she knows, she can't prove anything, can she?"

"Not a thing," said Grace, smiling.

XX

Kepple drove about the countryside, checking the hotels, the boarding-houses, the roadside inns.

"A tall girl, name of Salt. Might be calling herself Van Staden, that's her working title. She's an old friend, a visitor from overseas. She called to see us at the farm but we were out and missed her. We're anxious to get hold of her."

He met everywhere a flat, pale-eyed reticence. Often he was sure that the people he questioned were lying. The conviction grew in him that Emma Salt was known in these parts. After all, she must have lived somewhere since she arrived in England. Her nursing jobs had been spasmodic, she seemed to have independent means. Perhaps she had made Norfolk her headquarters when she was unemployed.

79

He set out to test the theory. His questions became more tricky. He bought a great many pints of beer for local drinkers, and was rewarded by looks of sly mockery, and nothing else. Kepple did not understand the folk of East Anglia, who having suffered several centuries of invasion and piracy, know a predator when they see one, and keep a still tongue.

At last, though, he came across a publican puffed up in his own conceit, who made the mistake of treating Kepple as a fool.

"You from London, sir?" he said, with a sideways look.

"That's right."

"Thinking of buying a House, mebbe? There's the Tricorn down Wensum way, has a good trade they say." The publican glanced round at his cronies for approval.

"I'm not interested in pubs for sale. I'm on holiday, staying on Mrs. Villiers' farm."

"Farm? Oh, you mean up at Oatham."

"Near there."

"Won't find any hotels that side. No tourists."

Kepple's head swung up smoothly. "No, that's true. But there are boats, aren't there? I hadn't thought of that."

The man looked taken aback. "Boats this time o' year? Bit nippy, I'd a' thought."

"Not for my friend, she's very hardy." Kepple was already sliding into his coat, grinning. "Thanks for giving me the idea."

As he hurried out, one of the men in the bar chuckled. "Shouldn't tease the tiger, Harry."

"Didn't tell 'im anything."

"She'll be wild at you."

"No, she won't." Harry began to collect glasses with a defiant rattle. "It's time. And I'll tell you one thing, he won't find her unless she wants. You can count on that."

XXI

THE CABIN-CRUISER was moored with several others alongside the breakwater at Oatham harbour. Kepple, looking down at the boats, reflected that they looked like working craft rather than luxury items, and wondered how it had been possible for Emma Salt to hire one.

There was no doubt that she had done so. The owner of the boat, run to earth in a local repair yard, admitted he had hired the boat to the girl. "Didn't want to at first, I don't mind saying. She seemed to know engines, though, and she's done a lot of sailing. She's capable, and the price was right."

This man was the sort, Kepple thought, who put price above all else. He had a bumpy red face and a thin reddish moustache. His fingers moved constantly in a faint pinching movement. Kepple made a mental note that he might be useful as a witness, some time.

"Is she aboard now?"

"Wouldn't know, I'm afraid."

"I have an important message for her."

"Go and take a look, why not? She'll be there, unless she's taken the *Britta* over the bar."

Kepple walked to the water's edge and along the quay. He found the *Britta* moored near the end. She was deserted, the cabin locked. He climbed along to peer through the ports. Everything in the cabin was very tidy, the lower bunk neatly made up. Various personal possessions were stowed about the place. Kepple, who knew nothing of boats, thought this one was in the care of someone who did.

He clambered back to the quay and looked about him. Oatham was a village that had once traded in wool, and fish. It still ran a few trawlers, but the configuration of the coast had altered over the centuries, and silting of the harbour was a constant problem. In summer, the sailing community provided a meagre source of income; but at this time of year, when the winds blew rough and cold inshore, most of the activity was in Oatham's two boat-yards, where the work of caulking, repairing and painting continued throughout the daylight hours.

To the west of the harbour lay marshy land. To the east, the shore was sandy. On the fringe of the village, an ancient groyne of rocks and earth thrust seawards at right-angles to the quay, and at the limit of the groyne stood a conical building with a steep roof, that Kepple took to be the ruins of a watch-tower. He thought it might provide a good climber with an admirable view of the coast in both directions.

There were a great many seabirds, gannets perhaps, scavenging round the harbour walls. Kepple lifted his head to watch them, fascinated by the white explosion of their wings as they turned in the sun, the sharp angling of their necks and legs as they braked and dropped. He stood so for a minute or two, and when he glanced back at the quay, Emma Salt was standing two paces from him.

For a moment he was so startled that he stood gaping. Then annoyance surged over him and he said, "where the hell were you hiding?"

She made no answer, merely tilting her head a little. The wind from the sea caught at her long, curling black hair, blowing it sideways across her face, and she put up a hand to brush it away.

He saw that his memory of her had been faulty; or perhaps she had decided at last to be seen, and cast aside some protective ambiguity. The face he saw now he would not forget. It was strongly boned, the cheekbones high yet rounded, the eyes large and brilliantly dark. She was tall, her bosom full under the black sweater she wore. She had the light, balancing stance of a fighter. Her black slacks were tucked into the top of short sea-boots, and between the fingers of her right hand he saw one of the small black cheroots favoured by some women on the Continent.

Kepple said uncertainly, "You are Emma Salt?"

Her eyes changed focus, as if she gazed not at him, but into him. It was a look that betrayed the creature capable of deliberate cruelty; and Kepple, who could be cruel himself, was instantly wary.

He said in a sharpened tone, "If you are Emma Salt, I want to talk to you."

"Talk away."

"Somewhere out of this wind would be more comfortable."

"The boat's in the lee of the breakwater." She stepped past him and led the way back to the *Britta*. She walked easily, swinging her feet rather wide because of the boots. When she reached the boat, which had already dropped some way with the fall of the tide, she swung down to the deck with practised grace. As Kepple followed, he said, "I'm told you're something of a sailor?"

She perched on the port rail. "I've done a bit."

"Where?"

She leaned over and flicked the butt of the cheroot into the water. "Japan, Malaysia, Sydney, West Indies, New England, Cornwall, Brittany."

"You're very well travelled."

"Yes." He had the feeling she was amused by his questions. There was a note of mockery in her voice; a strange voice, as Thiers had said, with a foreign lilt rather than an accent. There was a sudden glitter in the turn of the vowels, too, like the glitter of metal in quartz.

"And what has all this travel taught you?"

"Never to go the hard-arse way," she said. "I'm like you, Mr. Kepple. I like comfort. But then, like you I was a charity child."

Kepple's head jerked up, and she laughed.

"Did you think it was a secret? It's quite easy to trace the life history of a prominent citizen. You spent your childhood in a Birmingham tenement. When you were seven your father fell off a truckload of steel rods. The wheels went over his head and he lost the few brains he had. After that, it was the orphanage for you."

Kepple stared at her in silence for a moment; then his right hand described an uncertain movement, as if he brushed something aside. "I'm not ashamed of being a charity boy."

"No? Well, they did you proud, after all. Scholarship to grammar school, bursary to Cambridge. And you worked, Kepple man, you really polished the diamond. Even your voice. I admire you, the way you've made the top grade. You'd fool most people. Not the county, I suppose; and not the insiders like me who've been through the same hoops as you." She screwed up her eyes against the sun which was now full overhead. "We can recognise the charity smell. It's like old sweat in a jersey, you never get it out." Suddenly she leaned towards him. "Look at me, Kepple. Look at my eyes. You'll see yourself there. See? The charity kid, all dressed up in the gear that's made to last. Washed in grey soap, shut up at night behind grey walls, thinking grey thoughts. So when the good times come, we know how to appreciate them. Walter Kepple and Emma Salt, two of a kind." She kicked out a leg and studied the toe of the boot. "Done very well for yourself, haven't you?"

"So, it appears, have you."

"Fair to middling."

"How, may one ask?"

"Nursing the rich old slobs of the world."

"There's money in that?"

"Yes, if you're a good nurse. I am. You choose someone who's old and sick, very sick, but clear in the head. You're good to them. They see you right. The West Indies is a fine place to work. Plenty of luxury cruises and millionaires' houses. Half of them eat and drink too much, and most of them are scared of death. He's the one old codger they can't buy off. You help them fool death a while, and they shell out."

"Leave you money, too, I suppose?"

"Sometimes. That's why I said, choose someone clear in the head, otherwise the relatives'll try and get the legacy withdrawn. Amazing how many people will swear their near and dear were insane, when the will is read to them."

Kepple was sitting facing her now. There was something extraordinarily compelling about her. It was not only the braggart air, it was something deeper; an impression she gave of totality. She would make any emotion absolute, absolute boredom, entire absorption with the hunt, unrestrained love or hate, unswerving purpose. Against his will, Kepple found himself drawn to her. He literally shook his head, as if to dispel her image, and said, "Emma Salt is a most unusual name, isn't it?"

"It's not my only one."

"So I gather. Is Van Staden your correct name?"

"Time will tell, Mr. Kepple."

"Unfortunately, I haven't time to spare. I came here to discuss a specific question, Miss Salt. You have a sunburst brooch to sell. Can I see it?"

Again she laughed. "I'm afraid not. Are you thinking of making an offer?"

"It's unlikely. I'm not interested in jewellery."

"Ah? Then how about Adam. Is he interested, do you think?"

"He finds your approach a little tiresome. Melodrama and business don't mix well, in my view. But for what it's worth, he seems to be taking your wish to sell as genuine."

"It's genuine all right."

"And what about the brooch?"

She smiled. "You'll judge for yourself how genuine that is."

"M. Thiers never offered to buy it."

"I told him it wasn't for sale to him. And it's not for sale to you, Kepple."

"Who then? Adam Villiers?"

"Perhaps. Perhaps his mother. Perhaps she'll tell Adam to buy it."

"Adam makes his own decisions."

"That's not what people tell me."

"Believe what you like." Kepple shrugged. "Where did you get the brooch? Was it the gift of a grateful patient?"

"It was left me."

"So one presumes the patient died?"

"Yes. Dead as a doornail. The brooch belongs to me, for richer for poorer, for better for worse, till death do us part. Or a good price. The Villiers family should be able to give me a good price, don't you think?"

Kepple shifted his position, so that the warm wood of the cabin pressed his back. "Take my advice, Miss Salt. Don't try and be smart. If you are making an honest offer, go to Adam and talk."

"Honest?" She appeared to ponder the word, then looked up with a smile. "I'm honest with honest men. With you, I'll be half-honest. With cheats and liars, I may cheat and lie. Does that seem fair?"

"It's fair warning."

"And now, run home and tell Grace all about it."

"Will you still be here tomorrow?"

"Perhaps. I please myself."

He stood up, placed a foot on the *Britta*'s rail, reached for a stanchion high in the stone wall, and pulled himself up to the quayside. Standing there, he looked back at the woman and said in a soft voice, "Tell me one thing, Miss Salt? Did you kill the owner of that brooch?"

For a second her face went completely blank. Gazing at that stony mask, at the parted lips and lightless eyes, Kepple was suddenly afraid; as if, striking at some mortal target, he had found himself full in the gaze of the implacable goddess of vengeance.

XXII

"She's mad. Obsessed." Kepple faced Adam and Matt across the empty dining-table. Grace and Zoe were out walking, and the house held the stillness of three in the afternoon. "There's something about her smile." He ran a hand over his own mouth. "Matt, can you remember, was anyone killed in the course of the Kostroma robbery?"

"No-one."

"You sure?"

"Yes. I'm also sure the robbery has nothing to do with Villiers Glass." Matt's voice was unequivocal. "I checked the facts. Before we left London I went round to the *Gazette*. The Crime Editor is a friend of mine. He's been on the paper since the year One. There's not much on record about the Kostroma case. The truck of valuables was hijacked by conspiracy, that was clear. The driver was mixed up in it. There was no bloodshed. The police in a dozen countries failed to get a sniff of the jewels or the thieves. Nobody ever suggested there might be a homicide charge attached. Why d'you ask?"

"Somebody connected with that brooch died by violence," said Kepple flatly, and as Matt's head wagged in scepticism, he repeated, "you didn't see her face, Matt. I did."

"You think Emma Salt's responsible for some murder?"

"I didn't say that. I think someone died, and she either knows the killer or thinks she knows."

"You said yourself we needed facts, not guesses."

"Her reaction was a fact."

"Not in the legal sense."

"Wait." Adam bent forward to interrupt them. "Wally, could you make a guess at her nationality?"

"Hard to tell." Kepple frowned in thought. "Her English is correct, idiomatic. Rather racy. Her intonation is a little unusual."

"Would you say English is her first language?"

Again Kepple hesitated. "Now, yes, I would. But I rather think she might have had a different mother tongue, as a child. Something that left that very faint mark on her voice. She's lived in a good many places, if she was telling the truth."

"Such as?"

"West Indies, the States, the Far East."

"Anything else she told you?"

"Yes. She was in some sort of Institution, as a child."

"We might be able to trace that."

"We might."

There was a brief silence. They heard, far off, the lazy bump of breakers on the shore.

Matt said slowly, "And you think she genuinely plans to sell the brooch?"

"I don't doubt it for a moment," said Kepple. "I'll tell you something else. The price she sets on it will be ruinous."

"You're not chilled?" Kepple took one of Grace's hands, bent forward to kiss the cheeks that glowed with delicate colour. "You haven't tired yourself?"

"Heavens no. It was only a little stroll to the beach. I feel better for it."

He bent and added two big logs to the fire that burned on her bedroom hearth. She moved towards it and said, "Adam tells me you found the woman?"

"Yes." He stood up to face her and she smiled.

"Victor in the chase. What's she like?"

"Striking in a wild-cat sort of way. Dark and tall, with very dark eyes. Dangerous. I shouldn't think she's ever been afraid in her life. Or rather, she has the look of someone who's

87

never met her match."

"We must give her that experience."

Wally grinned. "You're really something, aren't you?"

"Mmh."

He moved forward and took her in his arms, brushed his lips lightly against her forehead, spoke almost to himself. "The one source of reason in a mad world. My world, anyway."

She stood quietly leaning against him. "Since when have you needed help?"

"I don't know. I do need it. I'm growing old."

"Nonsense."

"Grace? Marry me?"

"Oh . . . Wally dear."

"Why not? Why not?"

She stood back from him and he let her go, watching her slip the tweed coat from her shoulders, drop it on her bed, sit down at the dressing-table and pull the pins from her high coil of hair. She loosened it with her fingers; picked up a brush and began to wield it with slow and languid strokes.

"All right." Wally moved to the chair close by her. "This other thing, this Emma Salt. I can't do anything more to help you until you confide in me."

"There's nothing I can tell you, Wally."

"Tell me the truth. You told Adam and Boyle about that nursing agency. Why not me?"

"It slipped my mind. I wasn't well, remember. I'm sorry if I hurt your feelings."

"Hurt!" There was so much misery in his voice that she turned round on the seat to face him.

"Wally, it's not a case of what I want to do. There are some secrets that are . . . that are not one's own to reveal."

"You mean you're protecting someone?"

"Yes."

"Who?"

She made no reply. Her gaze shifted back to the looking-glass, her arm took up its rhythmic movement. He sat watching her, thinking that no matter how much he loved her and how much he did for her, she would never let him share her thoughts. Her body she gave, but the mind, the confidence for which he hungered, she withheld. It was, he thought bitterly, the ultimate mark of the harlot. It turned their relationship into dead sea fruit. When he first became her lover, he had believed that the act of love was the expression of love. Now he knew that each act was a measure of how little she loved him.

"Henry," he said to her, "are you looking after Henry still?"

Her head moved faintly, but he could not know whether she denied the accusation or the rage that prompted it.

"I can never give you anything," he said in a low voice, "no-one can ever give you anything. Why won't you allow . . . ?"

"Wally." She swung round on the stool, setting down the brush. "Please don't."

"Don't what? Love you? What do you want me around for, because I'm good in bed, because I control seven votes on the Board?" He came towards her. "It's not enough, it's not good enough. You know what that woman said? The charity stamp shows. All those years of charity I took, the worst of it was having nothing to give. You know that?"

She stared up at him with wide eyes. "What are you talking about?"

"The worst was having nothing that anyone on God's earth wanted. Nothing to give. At Christmas nothing, at Easter nothing. A perfect and a contrite heart, some of them had that, but not me. I had nothing to give to God nor man and I still have nothing. Don't you understand, Grace? I can't be a charity boy any longer."

"Wally? Wally!"

"No." He struck aside the hand she raised to him.

"My dearest, please."

"Don't use that whore's trick."

She rose and walked towards her wardrobe. "We'd better talk later."

"Later? From now on I'm looking after myself."

She opened the cupboard and lifted out a dress. "The Kepple rule."

"The Kepple rule for the Villiers game. I learned it from a good mistress."

She glanced round, but he was already thrusting out of the room. The door closed with a snap.

Grace dropped the dress on a chair. She went quickly to the dressing-table, bent forward, twisted her hair up and jabbed in pins to hold it. Her hands touched the flesh under her eyes. She reached for powder, applied a little lipstick, rubbed Cologne on her wrists. As she straightened up, Zoe hurried into the room.

"Grace, what have you done to Wally?"

"Nothing at all. He's got some tantrum."

But Zoe's eyes were bright with panic. "You fool, Grace. Now, of all times. You absolute fool."

XXIII

On the night of January 4th there was a strong wind, but by morning it had dropped and the weather was warmer. Adam woke to the cry of gulls moving seaward, returning, circling. He got up and dressed, and went outside. The birds were over the beach, flying low. Their shadows flicked the dunes that shone with an ivory glaze under the early sun. He took the path between them, emerged on the long slope of the beach, and saw Emma Salt.

She was far down, near the water line. Her black jeans were rolled up to the calf, and she was running bent over, her left hand trailing a stick. As Adam drew closer, he saw that she was writing her first name in huge letters. Above her, the gulls wheeled. There was something witchlike in the intensity of her concentration. She finished the tail of the "a" with a ritual flourish, and only then straightened and looked at Adam.

He stopped a few paces from her. "My name is Adam Villiers."

"I know." She stood motionless against the incessant motion of the waves, staring at him with the same extraordinary intentness, as if she compared him with some mental image.

He thought he had seldom seen such avid, sucking curiosity. She gazed as if she would draw the soul out of him. He felt more strongly than ever the force of her personality. Her face expressed a flamboyant arrogance. Like Lucifer fallen she dwarfed with her sullen presence the huge tumble of clouds above her and the immense sweep of the sands to east and west. If she raised her arm, he felt, the sea-birds might swoop to attack him, the storm winds mutter again in the far corners of the sky.

He shook himself, and said aloud, "A few centuries ago, they'd have burned you at the stake."

"They still try," she said, and turned her gaze from him. "Are you afraid of the evil eye?"

"No, only of human agencies."

"Kepple was afraid, yesterday."

"You wanted him afraid, didn't you? Perhaps he feared your will to be feared."

"And you don't?" She turned back, her eyes shining.

"I think I can beat you at your own game."

"You don't know my game."

"The game of fear. One must have confidence in one's own hand."

"Aha," she moved a little closer to him and her teeth showed in excited laughter, "but you won't be allowed to play your hand. Kepple and the rest will play it for you, and they'll lose."

"Kepple may try. My mother is out of the game. She's ill."

"Not dead yet, though."

"For a nurse you have a strange attitude to suffering."

"I was ill, as a child." She bent her right leg and pointed to a number of silvery circles on the shin and ankle. "Those come from malnutrition. I was covered in sores. My dress stuck to my body. My hair fell out."

"Which camp were you in?"

Her gaze flickered. "Find out. Let Boyle find out. I didn't come here to answer your questions."

"Then why did you come, Emma?"

"Why d'you think?" He understood that she was not merely

being impertinent, but was eager to discover how much he already knew.

"You came," he said, "because you can't keep away. The persecutor can't expect to be free of his victims. You can't be free of us."

She scowled, and he bent and picked up the stick she had dropped. "Tell me, what made you choose a name like Salt? Was it because you love the sea?"

As she made no answer, he ran his hand along the smooth curve of the stick. "Grey and smooth as silk," he said. "That is the work of salt, you know. It sinks into the wood, dries it out and makes it smooth and hard. Emma Salt. The salt of tears, is that what you are? The salt rubbed in the wound?"

Still she was silent, listening with bent head.

"Or perhaps the salt of the earth? No?" He lifted the stick higher, holding it at shoulder level. His voice was soft, caressing. "Look at it. Flotsam from the sea. A lovely shape, though. Look at that line? I could have it gilded for you, set with pearls, the sea's own jewel. I could make it a wand worth the waving. A wand to command great wealth, to conjure up the treasure ships, to call the sleeping djinn from the heart of the glass. I could show you a certain magic, Emma."

"I don't use magic. I don't need it."

"No? No sirens, no Neptune in that ocean? Not even Davy Jones with a locker full of rubies and dead men's bones?"

"What do you mean?"

"You only believe in the sorcery of the twentieth century? Frightening a sick woman, just for the hell of it?"

"She had it coming."

"So at least you believe in Nemesis?"

"What?"

"What gods do you light your fire for? Who answers when you knock on wood?"

"I'm not superstitious."

"Do you believe in God?"

"No."

"Do you have a moral code, an ethical system?"

"I know what I want and I go for it. I don't hurt the innocent."

92

"So you have a method of defining innocence? What is it?"

"I know what I want," she repeated. She shifted round in the sand so that she faced him. She was angry, but caught by his questions.

"You know what you want today, but it could be something else the next day, ten years hence?"

"Now is all the time we have."

"Then that's your system. A blind submission to the urgency of the moment. What you want now, you fight for. Tomorrow, if the wind changes, you fight as hard to undo what you have done. You have the determination and immediacy and the joylessness of a rat in a maze."

"I get my kicks."

"I'm sure you do."

"I live."

"Certainly. From impulse to impulse. From day to day. Without empathy and without guilt. The definition of a psychopath."

"Listen." She was moving rapidly towards him. "You're right. I live from day to day. From hour to hour. From breath to breath if I have to. You wouldn't understand that sometimes all that matters is the next breath. You wouldn't know."

"I've not had your experience of life . . . or death."

"Perhaps it's time you learned."

"Do you mean to teach me?"

She burst out laughing. "That I do. You'll be in experienced hands, you and the rest of your pack. Now I'll tell you, I came here because it's time to talk about the brooch."

"Tired of the cupboard under the stairs? All right, out you come. Where's the brooch?"

"I haven't got it here. I'll show it to you in good time."

"Which is?"

"January 12th." The answer came without hesitation. "I'll come to your mother's flat at Glass House. Eight o'clock."

"And what," he said lightly, "if we have the place surrounded with policemen, ready to pounce on you? What, in more mundane circumstances, if one of us has another engagement? All sorts of things spring to my mind."

But she had regained her composure. "You'll all come. She'll see to that."

He nodded. "I'll take your word for it. M. Thiers priced the brooch at £275. What's your starting price?"

"You must see it before we bargain."

"Right. One last thing. You told Wally Kepple that Salt isn't your only name. What is the real one? Do I introduce you as Salt, or Van Staden?"

"Better ask Phillip Boyle."

She turned away from him and walked off along the hard sand at the sea's edge. He let her go. She walked easily, without glancing to left or right. After a while, her form seemed almost to float on the bright gold dazzle of the water. He sighed and glanced down at the name she had traced on the beach. Already a high-running wave had blurred the foot of the letters. Small discs of water lay in the curve of the "e" and the "a". Adam stretched out his arm, and with the stick he still held, began to write a "V".

Someone shouted. Walter Kepple came hurrying between the dunes. As he approached Adam he said breathlessly, "That woman. Who was she?"

"Emma Salt," said Adam.

"What did she want?"

"To meet us, to discuss the sale of the brooch. We agreed on the date, January 12th, at the penthouse."

"Bloody cheek. But by that time we'll have something against her."

"Maybe, although I think she's probably immune from prosecution. My impression is that she knows she's safe."

Kepple's gaze dropped to the writing in the sand. "She may feel safe without being safe. She admitted to me that a number of the people she nursed died. Certainly she stole that card while she was looking after Grace. She uses two names. No, to my mind, Emma Salt or Emma Van Staden is at best a thief and a fraud."

"Thief, yes. Fraud, I'm not so sure. I wish I thought her fraudulent. A genuine witch is far more alarming than a fake one."

"Think she may turn us all into toads?"

Adam swung back his arm and flung the stick far out to sea. It struck the water upright and seemed to dance for a moment before it sank. "I think she may prove that we've been toads all along."

"Don't treat her lightly."

"No. I think it's time to get back to London and see what Boyle's managed to turn up."

Kepple grunted. "Can't be too soon for me."

XXIV

ADAM COLLECTED A plate of bacon and eggs from the kitchen and went to join Matt in the breakfast room.

"You're up early." The old man pointed to the coffee pot beside him. "That stuff's undrinkable, don't touch it. Where's Wally?"

"Gone into the village to send a cable. I want Boyle back in London as soon as he can make it. Would you mind if we left here today?"

"Mind? I'll be glad to shake the mud of Norfolk from my shoes."

"Matt," Adam sat down at the table, "is there the smallest chance that either of my parents could have been involved in the Kostroma robbery?"

"Good God, no." Matt's head swung back and forth in furious impatience. "Are you out of your mind?"

"No, I don't think so." Adam took an envelope from his pocket and spread the contents before Matt. "Take a look."

"What are these?"

"Photographs of the Kostroma brooch, stolen in 1939. Old Thiers had the illustration in a book. He allowed me to photograph it. The prints reached me yesterday."

"And what's it supposed to prove?"

"Compare this with the prints." Adam took out the card that Emma Salt had left in the foyer on Christmas night.

Matt put on his spectacles, picked up the card and the clearest print, and turned to the light. He examined the two articles for some time, then laid them aside and looked at Adam thoughtfully."

"They match," he agreed.

"That drawing," said Adam, "isn't a Christmas decoration, but a diagram of the Kostroma brooch. I spotted the likeness when Thiers showed me the illustration in Paris."

"So?" Matt's eyes remained fixed on Adam's face, his thick fingers stroked the edge of the table.

"In the last two years of his life," continued Adam, "my father was busy making replica jewellery. He imported workers from Holland to help him, Lisbet Jonkers being one of these. Each time a replica was completed, an index card was drawn for it, and numbered by my father. This card is numbered 183. The inference seems to be that it was drawn by Zoe, who scrawled the words, 'Happy Christmas, Henry darling,' across the reverse face. That would set the making of the replica brooch at somewhere near Christmas 1936, because in mid-January of 1937 my father left home for good."

"Sounds reasonable."

"To sum up; by Christmas 1936, my father had completed a series that included at least 183 fake jewels. What I want to know is, did that series represent the entire Kostroma collection? Think of it, Matt. A replica collection could be used to replace the genuine pieces in the family safe while the real gems were disposed of secretly. Later, when the stones had been safely dispersed, a 'robbery' of the copies could be staged, and compensation claimed from the insurance companies. Perhaps that's the way the Kostroma collection was 'stolen'. That would explain why the police found no trace of the jewels, or of any hijack team. In other words, the true Kostroma robbery could have taken place gradually in the years preceding 1939. When war broke out, it provided the perfect opportunity to stage the fake, cover robbery."

"And you suggest your father deliberately connived at this plan?"

"It seems possible."

"It bloody doesn't." Matt hunched his shoulders like a

sighting buffalo. "People don't index their criminal actions and leave the cards around for anyone to find. I don't even know if it's legal to make duplicates of a valuable article without telling your insurance company; but I'm dead sure that if Henry made that replica, he did it legally. Plenty of respectable families have copies made of heirlooms. The Kostroma family may be no exception. And there's nothing to show Henry made more than the one brooch for them. The rest of the index could refer to a whole string of replicas of individual jewels, each for a different customer."

"Matt, I don't like making these suggestions, but I want to consider the sort of threat we may have to face. It seems probable that fake brooch was made with my father's help. He may have been honest, but what about Lisbet? She came over to England in a batch of immigrants whom no-one knew. She'd worked in Amsterdam, one of the biggest centres of illicit as well as legal traffic in gems. In late 1936, about the time that card was drawn, Lisbet and my father returned from a holiday that took them to the Continent and to North Africa. At that time a good many illicit jewel deals were worked through Casablanca. There was plenty of opportunity for my father to get mixed up in some crook deal, knowingly or not."

Matt thrust the prints from him with an angry sweep. "Now that's drivel, Adam. Your dad was a fool, but not that sort of fool. He used his eyes and ears more than most. And he wouldn't have touched anything dirty, you can stake your lot on that."

"He was in love with a woman who might have been a crook."

"She didn't have the brains, damn it. She was a half-baked, thriftless little Dutch dolly, and nobody in his right mind would have let her near any business, straight or crooked. She'd have balled up the simplest plan in five seconds flat."

"She collaborated with the Germans during the war."

"Yes, by lying flat on her back, and if that makes her a criminal, then the world's gaols aren't big enough. Don't feed me garbage about Henry Villiers. It's not sensible or decent for you to think it, let alone say it."

"I don't necessarily believe it, Matt. All I know is that the fake Kostroma brooch concerns us somehow, or Emma Salt wouldn't have left that card in the foyer. Another point. I'm darn sure Zoe remembers all about the card. If there's nothing dishonest, why doesn't she tell us what she knows? Why doesn't she admit the card is a picture of the brooch? She's said nothing, even though she knows I've spoken to Thiers, even though Thiers told me Emma Salt has a fake Kostroma to sell."

"Zoe's a liar by long habit."

"And my mother? Why has she said nothing?"

"Perhaps she never knew of the replica, or the card."

"She must have known. The card must have been drawn before my father left her. Zoe would surely have told her about it. And if it was stolen from my mother's flat, she certainly knew it was there. I'm convinced we're not being told the truth."

"Well, you won't get them to change their tune now. Grace won't discuss anything that throws an ill light on Henry, and Zoe will do as Grace bids. Don't waste your time on them."

"No. We'll have to hope that Boyle comes up with something. There's one other line we must follow up, and that's Wally's idea that Emma Salt has lived in the Far East. There's something on the tip of my tongue, a name, or something I should remember."

"Ask Halstead. He spent twenty years out there. He still deals with all the Far East contracts, and he's got a memory like an elephant."

"I'll see him." Adam got to his feet. "Now I'm going to pack. Wally's going to tell Mother we're needed urgently on the Buenos Aires prospect. With any luck we'll be back in London by lunch-time, and we can talk to Boyle directly he reaches Glass House."

XXV

WHEN THEY REACHED London, however, they found that bad

weather had closed several airports on the Continent, including Schiphol. Boyle telephoned to say they might expect him on the early morning flight on January 6th.

Matt accordingly went off to inspect new machinery that was to be installed in the fibre-glass factories, Wally went into conference on the Annual Report, and Adam sought out Halstead.

He was the second-in-command of the Legal Department, a small, frail man with a nervous blink and a rather high-pitched voice. Some smart aleck in P.R. had once called Halstead "the ass with the delicate air." This man was now pushing soap in the provinces, while Halstead was certain to head his department in a year or two. He had an incisive mind, an incredible memory, and he got on well with people. He sat now, dwarfed by a desk as wide as a billiard table, and listened to Adam with grave courtesy.

"So you want to know," he said, at the end, "whether I can recall anything about refugees or prison camps in the Far East, relating to a person or persons named Van Staden, or Salt. That is a very tall order. Van Staden is a not uncommon Dutch name. There were several with me in my own camp. Really, Adam, your best plan would be to apply to the proper Government department, and even then it would be looking for a needle in a haystack."

"I'm thinking of a cause célèbre," said Adam. "Something like that case, do you remember, the girl who was brought up by an Indonesian nanny, and then reclaimed by the parents?"

"Ah yes, I know the case you mean. But that didn't involve anyone by the name of Salt, or Van Staden. Of course, there may have been a number of similar situations which did not become causes célèbres. Many people lost children when the Far East was over-run by the Japanese, and such people often followed up all manner of hopeless trails. I don't recall . . ." Halstead suddenly stopped speaking and stared at the ceiling. "No, no, wait a moment. Oh goodness me, of course, yes. Salt. Salt is the key word. There was a very sad case, a man named Li Abas, in Java. The poor man fostered a child for six years, and came up against

99

a couple of misbegotten missionaries called Salt. It was not a question of a claim by the parents. It was a question of whether the child should be left where it was, or removed to the care of people of its own race and religion. I always thought the authorities reached quite the wrong decision."

"Have you records? Could you look them up?"

"I've nothing here, but I could certainly find the reference in my own library at home. Is it urgent?"

"Most. And confidential."

"I see. Well, Adam, let me get what I can for you in the course of the next hour or so. I'll send young Jubber out to my place, with a note to my wife. I'll let you know as soon as he's brought what I have to offer."

"Thank you, Bob." Adam stood up, but before he left the room he asked one more question.

"Can you remember whether this Li Abas story involved a brooch?"

"That I'm afraid I can't remember. If there was a brooch, then it was not given great publicity in the Press. However, I'll see what I can find."

"I'll be in my office," said Adam; and going there, told Miss Fergusson to make no further appointments for him that afternoon, and to admit no-one except Mr. Halstead.

XXVI

AT FIVE O'CLOCK, as the clerks and typists began to pour out of the doors of Glass House, and the traffic along the river banks set up a constant high droning, Halstead appeared in the door of Adam's office.

He was carrying several books, marked with strips of paper, and he came across and dumped them on Adam's desk.

"You were quite right," he said happily, "the names Van Staden and Salt both appear. I think it will be clearer if I relate the story to you without too much reference to the legal arguments. I take it you are interested in the tale as a tale, rather than as a legal battle?"

Adam nodded, and Halstead drew up a chair, leaned his

elbows on the desk, and began:

"Li Abas was a man of mixed blood, part Chinese, part Javanese. He lived in a tiny village in extremely rough country. He was ill-educated and worked as a labourer on various estates, where he picked up a certain amount of Holland's Dutch and English. In 1947, Li Abas approached a Dutchman named Reunert, who was a merchant in Cheribon, a small coastal town. Li had a brooch to sell. He said someone had given it to him during the 'bad years', meaning when the island was under Japanese occupation. He asked Reunert what the brooch would fetch. Reunert examined the thing, decided it might be stolen goods, and told the police. They asked Li Abas a great many questions. He stuck to his story. He had been given the brooch by a Dutch couple, hiding from the Japanese, in exchange for food and clothing. He maintained he had protected these people as long as he could, but eventually their hiding-place had been discovered by Japanese troops, and they had been taken away to a prison camp. Now times were bad, work was hard to find, and he was forced to sell the brooch in order to exist."

Halstead paused, and drew forward a second book. "There things might have rested, had not the merchant mentioned to the police that the workmanship of the brooch was unusually good, and it might be possible to trace its origin. At that, Li Abas became hysterical. He demanded the immediate return of his property, and attempted to snatch the brooch from Reunert. There was a scuffle, a policeman was slightly injured, and Li Abas spent the night in the town lock-up.

"A new phase now opened. You will recall that at this period, Java was in a state of great unrest, the Javanese seeking to expel the Dutch colonial power. The police officer in Cheribon was a Hollander. His opposite number in Li's home district was not. The two got across each other. Li's man said Li was a patriot who must be released from custody forthwith. He further stated that Li needed money to support his daughter, that his visit to Cheribon was honestly motivated, and that if he did not return home quickly, the child must suffer.

"This ultimatum made the commandant in Cheribon turn stubborn. He demanded that the Mission Station in the interior confirm the existence and the condition of the child in question; and on to the stage tripped, not to say blundered, Dr. and Mrs. Jacob Salt.

"These two zealots were precisely the sort of persons who should never be allowed to undertake any kind of mission, religious or secular. They appear to have had a predilection for grasping the inessential and ignoring all else. Quite devoid of humour and understanding, they lived by a set of principles so rigid that even their own sect found them impossible, and lost no time in shipping them out of Sydney to the remote areas of Java.

"It was these people who were called on to deal with a situation that needed above everything a freedom from prejudice, and a more than ordinary warmth of heart.

"The Salts went to the house of Li Abas in his absence and talked to, or at, the child. She did not talk to them, which is understandable; but the Salts formed the opinion that she was mentally retarded. They also decided she was of Caucasian descent . . . what we in our haphazard way call 'white'. The child had few clothes, they said, and was receiving no religious instruction. They did not add that clothes in that climate are often superfluous, and that the child was being instructed in the Buddhist faith. I must emphasise that despite his personal shortcomings, Jacob Salt was a doctor of medicine, and a student of anthropology, so his opinion carried some weight in certain quarters."

Halstead leaned back in his chair and tapped one hand on the desk. "So you see, two struggles were now in progress. The first to prove that Li Abas had stolen the brooch, the second to prove he had stolen the child.

"On the first issue, I would say that Li Abas told the truth when he claimed the brooch was given him in payment for services rendered. He stated that the two Dutch citizens, named Van Staden, had at the time of Japanese invasion sought refuge near his village. He had shown them a place to hide in the mountains near by, had kept them supplied with food and information, and in return had received the brooch. This story could not be disproved. There had been numerous people named Van Staten or Van Staden among the captives herded about Java, and many of them had died or vanished without it being recorded by authority. These two were never traced, but it seems likely that they did not survive the war years.

"Li Abas could not be charged with the theft of the brooch. His real struggle was to keep the child. He said at first that she was Javanese, that the mother was dead and he was the rightful father. His village supported this statement. But every community has its Judas, and his was no exception. A man was at last found who said the girl was not Li's child but the child of a white couple, whom Li had robbed and betrayed to the Japanese.

"Again, the weight of evidence was in Li's favour, and things might have simmered down if left alone, but the Salts were aflame with missionary fervour. They were set upon saving the girl from a life of heathen degradation. They intended to make an educated White Christian of her, and they pulled in a lot of big guns on their side.

"Blood tests showed that Li Abas could not be the natural father of the child. Under prolonged questioning by people far better equipped with authority and learning than he, he became frightened and confused. He admitted the child was not born to him. He said first that she was a Javanese orphan, and later that she was the Van Stadens' child. He said they had managed to leave her hidden when they were captured, and that he had taken her and reared her as his own ever since.

"Clearly Li Abas was devoted to the child and she to him. Neither of them dreamed that by telling the truth they were endangering their future together.

"There began one of those tragi-farcical episodes that seem to afflict only the civilised races. The fight for the custody of the child blew up into a much-publicised issue. Governments, refugee organisations, and the Press attempted to trace the Van Stadens who might have been in Java at that time. I may add that two years later, no couple of that name and with a daughter of the right age had been traced. The theory developed that the villagers and Li had been mistaken in the name 'Van Staden'. But nothing could be proved.

"The Salts, meanwhile, began a legal drive to remove the child from Li Abas and place her in 'a proper Christian home'. They actually stated that they were prepared to adopt her themselves. Li, now completely bewildered and terrified, tried to abscond with the child. They eluded capture for some time, and when they were caught the child was underfed and ill. The Salts made great play of this. They emphasised the unsuitability of Li Abas as a parent. A Calvinist magistrate removed the child from Li and placed her in the care of the Salts. Nobody seems to have taken the trouble to explain to Li Abas that he could take legal action to defend his claim to custody.

"The child was kept more or less a prisoner in the Mission Station. Li Abas haunted the place, hoping to see her. After some weeks had passed, he came to see Mrs. Salt. She told him there was nothing he could do, the child was no longer his, and he must resign himself to the inevitable. He did. He gave the brooch into the safe-keeping of Mrs. Salt, went back to his house, and hanged himself.

"When the child learned what had happened, she ran away. She was recaptured . . . I would say that is the right word . . . and shipped to Australia in the care of the Salts. They were English themselves, and they intended to bring the girl home with them when their tour of duty in the Far East ended. During the next two months they tried to make the child their own, both in the legal and the social sense, but she would have none of them. She would not speak to them, existed in silence, refused to eat their food or accept their advances. If they took their eyes off her for an hour, she attempted to run away. At last she came before the courts again. This time there was a probation officer and a judge with some sense. They talked to the girl and elicited from her the statement that the Salts had killed her father, and she would never live with them. She asked to be returned to Java. The court decided that while this was impossible, she obviously could not remain with the Salts. She was placed in an orphanage. The case, as far as the world was concerned, was closed."

Halstead sighed. "It's an ugly story, but you must remember that at that time the world was not itself. We were still reeling under the shock of Belsen, Buchenwald and the like. There was a dreadful list of displaced and missing persons, half Europe was still occupied by foreign powers, and individuals like the child we're discussing did get pushed around by well-meaning idiots."

"You think she should have stayed with Li Abas, in the legal sense as well as the human?"

"Yes. The child loved the man, and he loved her. In their own eyes they were father and daughter. There was nothing, to my mind, that was Christian or civilised in the way the Salts broke up their home. It was a violation, a series of outrageous acts. One wonders how she survived such a series of blows to her personality."

Adam sat silent for a time, and then said, "Can you tell me one more thing? How did it come she kept the name of Salt?"

"Well, she would not have been registered, I expect, in Java. When she was moved to Australia, I expect they made a Late Registration of Birth. At that time the Salts were hoping to adopt her. Probably they suggested she be registered in their name. But even if it was not a legal registration, Salt is still her name if she was consistently known by it, and accepted it as her signature. In other words, one can establish an identity by long usage, that is legally acceptable. She is 'known as Salt', I have no doubt."

"But she could have changed her name by deed poll?"

"Yes."

"To Van Staden, for instance?"

"Yes." Halstead's shrewd eyes rested on Adam. "But that would not add a feather of weight to the evidence of Li Abas, you know. It wouldn't change her legal status. After all, a woman can call herself Victoria Regina, she can take the name by deed poll and make it her legal signature. But that does not alter the facts of her birth, it does not entitle her to lay claim to the Crown Jewels. A rose by any other name remains the same."

When Halstead had gone, Adam sat thinking for some time. At last he roused himself, and put through a telephone call to Phillip Boyle in Amsterdam.

XXVII

BOYLE ARRIVED AT Glass House at ten fifteen on January 6th, and was taken straight to Adam's office. There Adam recounted to him, Matt and Wally the conversations held with Mr. Halstead.

"So we can assume," said Kepple at the end, "that Emma Salt knows all about the Li Abas case, and is trying to prove that she was the child involved."

"She has possession of the brooch," said Matt.

"That means nothing. She could have got hold of both story and brooch at any point in her career. She's travelled a good deal, she's sharp-witted and capable of taking infinite pains. Look at the way she's studied our background. She could have done the same with that old Java history. Perhaps she was in that orphanage with the genuine Li Abas girl, perhaps she's met her in adult life. What matters at the moment is, how do we fit into the picture?"

"The brooch is the obvious link," said Adam.

"Exactly. She's made that quite plain. I told you the thing had a disreputable history, and I was right. It wouldn't surprise me in the least to find she did in the rightful owner."

"What I don't understand," said Matt, "is why the Press didn't make more of the fact that the Li Abas brooch was a replica of the Kostroma. You'd think they'd have picked that up, human interest and so on. Don't the police send out notices of stolen jewels?"

"Don't forget that the Kostroma robbery took place just before the fall of France," answered Adam. "The theft wasn't big news then. And when the war ended, Java was in turmoil. It could well be that the police out there never connected the Li Abas brooch with the original Kostroma. Or perhaps they did, and thought it of no importance. After all, it was only a copy of the stolen brooch. It's even possible that they conferred with the French police and decided to keep that angle quiet."

"Any road," said Matt, "Li Abas and his troubles had nothing to do with Villiers Glass."

"Not directly," said Kepple.

"Not in any way."

Kepple shifted in his chair. "I think we need to check that very carefully. Is there any possibility of a link between our Company, and a person or persons named Van Staden, who may have gone to Java just before the war?"

Boyle said in his flat voice, "Perhaps I'd better report now, Mr. Villiers?"

Adam nodded, and Boyle took from his pocket a bundle of notes and placed them tidily on the table before him.

"I think Mr. Kepple's point is well taken. As a matter of fact, before I left for Holland, I took it on myself to look up the names of Glass House personnel, past and present. I couldn't find anyone by the name of Salt or Van Staden on the records. I then decided to check up on customers and agents. I concentrated particularly on the years 1935 to 1940, because that covered the last years of Mr. Henry Villiers' life and the first period of Mrs. Grace Villiers' widowhood. All along, I've thought that was the key time for my investigation.

"I found that the lists of major customers at that time included four Van Stadens, none of them living in Europe. I had better luck with the agents. Villiers' agents in Amsterdam turned out to be Messrs. G. J. Van Staden and W. R. Wijk.

"On Mr. Villiers' instructions, I went to Amsterdam and asked some questions about the firm. It no longer exists. Old Van Staden and his wife went to a Nazi prison-camp. He died there in 1942. She survived. When the camp was liberated, some old servant traced her and got her to Switzerland. The daughter Mina was living there with her husband, who's a banker in Berne. Mrs. Van Staden later had to be moved to a mental hospital. There were three Van Staden sons. Laurens, the oldest, joined the Free Dutch Navy and was killed when his ship struck a mine. He was unmarried and left no issue. Alex, the next son, worked for a rubber company in the East Indies. That caught my eye a bit. But though he was married, he had no kids, so he doesn't help us. Theo was the youngest of the family, only fifteen when war broke out. His parents shipped him off to the States in the nick of time. He fell with his bum in the butter, did well for himself and is now a big jeweller in New York. I wasn't able to find out much about him.

"The family seems to have been well-thought-of, both socially and in trade circles. Plain, solid people, and comfortably placed. Only thing against them was they were mean with money. Couldn't keep their servants or their office staff. But there's nothing to show they were dishonest." Boyle hesitated and shot an awkward glance at Adam.

"In other words," said Kepple smoothly, "it's extremely unlikely they ever heard of the Kostroma sunburst, let alone the replica."

"Extremely unlikely."

"And unlikely," said Adam with equal smoothness, "that they were selling the copy on my father's behalf?"

Boyle raised his head and looked straight at Adam. "I don't see the Van Stadens doing anything under the counter, sir. A stuffy lot by all accounts. What's more, if the Kostroma family did commission your dad to make the replica, then the thing belonged to them. It couldn't be disposed of without their say-so. I don't think your dad would have done anything shady."

"There's one point," said Matt quietly. "Henry died in 1939. Perhaps the replica was disposed of after that."

"It still wasn't Villiers' property," said Kepple.

"How do you know?" Matt gave Kepple a stare of frank dislike. "The Kostroma robbery happened in 1939, but before Henry died. The Kostroma family was in financial difficulties. Once the original brooch had been stolen, they might well have decided they'd no use for the copy. They could have let Henry buy it cheap. It happens all the time. It'd then be quite legal for Henry or his heirs to send the brooch to Amsterdam for sale. And old man Van Staden might just as easily have bought it for one of his women-folk. There's no need to put a criminal interpretation on every damn thing that happened, is there?"

Kepple nodded. "All right, let's accept there was nothing scaly in the deal. I still think that Boyle's on a wild goose chase. You can't tie these Van Stadens to the Li Abas case. Alex Van Staden, who went East, had no children. So Emma Salt is not their child. And if Li Abas was speaking the truth, the Van Stadens, the child and the brooch entered his life at one and the same time."

Boyle chose to ignore this challenge and addressed Adam, "There's another thing you should consider, Mr. Villiers. Your father's wife Lisbet went back to Holland after he died. She could have taken the brooch to Amsterdam and disposed of it there."

"Seems possible; but I doubt if we could prove it now." Adam glanced at the calendar on his desk. "Today is the 6th. We have nearly a week before we're due to meet Miss Salt. It seems to me that our next course of action must be to try and check with the surviving members of the Van Staden family. I'd like to suggest that we send Mr. Boyle to New York to approach Theo Van Staden. He's the only surviving brother, he might just remember something that would help us." He opened the folder before him and lifted out an envelope. "These are the photographs of the Kostroma, the card left by Emma Salt, and the picture you got from the nursing agency. Show them to Van Staden if you can. He might be able to make some contribution."

"Why?" asked Kepple. "I mean why should he?"

"He's a jeweller," said Adam mildly, and turned back to Boyle. "Did you find out the address of the sister in Berne?"

"Mina Gebhardt, 19 Lorindastrasse."

Kepple spoke impatiently. "It seems a great waste of time and money. What can you uncover that the police could not? Theo Staden will simply tell you that he was a school-boy at that time and can remember nothing. And the girl is now a hausfrau in Swiss suburbia. What do you hope to find there, for God's sake?"

But Adam was considering the photograph of Emma Van Staden in her nurse's uniform.

"Perhaps," he said, "I may find a family likeness."

XXVIII

BOYLE LEFT ENGLAND in sleet and reached New York on the tail of a blizzard. Although the city itself was clear of snow, the cold had immobilised land traffic in the environs, frozen stevedores to their television sets, and honed the tempers of union bosses to a fine cutting edge. The cabby who drove Boyle to his hotel on 44th Street, between 5th and 6th Avenues, appeared to be dying of bronchial pneumonia, and said he'd heard more storms were on the way.

Despite this chilly advent, Boyle was in excellent spirits. He liked New York, which he always viewed as a child views a giraffe, with disbelief and delight. He got a kick out of avoiding its money traps. No doubt Villiers Glass would have staked him to a classy hotel, but Boyle always chose this small place, which was clean, comfortable, and moderate. His one extravagance on expense account was his choice of a New York Agency. Runyan's, which he customarily used for all tie-in work in the States, charged top prices.

He put a call through to Runyan's as soon as he reached his hotel room. The boss, an old rock crystal named Carmichael, said that Villiers had already cabled their interest in the life and times of Theo Van Staden; and he went on to suggest that Boyle should talk to Torben Lindsall, a man Runyan's used for upper-crust society work. Switched through to Lindsall, Boyle agreed to meet him for lunch in an hour's time.

He then filled in time bathing and shaving and telephoning the office of Theo Van Staden. The latter, it turned out, was not in town. His secretary's voice implied that the best people knew this. Pressed for details, the woman said that he was Studying the Collections, clearly a form of spiritual retreat that was not to be disturbed even by fully-ordained jewellers. Boyle hinted that Villiers Glass was anxious to discuss costume jewellery with Mr. Van Staden. This chipped the ice a little, but did not melt it. After a moment's thought, Boyle murmured that Mr. Adam Villiers had recently shared a most interesting conversation with M. Eugène Thiers, of Paris, which he felt would merit the attention of Mr. Van Staden.

Thiers plus Villiers equalled thaw. The secretary, with the air of one tossing rosebuds, said she would try to get a message to her employer. Boyle arranged to ring back at three o'clock.

He then made for the Kitcat, and once past the frozen sludge outside it, and a frightening array of Episcopalian matrons in the hall, he reached a bar exactly to his taste. It was warm, brightly lit, and equipped with the right liquors. Lindsall was already there. He was a tall, narrow man, of Swedish extraction, with a high bumpy forehead and pale silver eyes that exactly matched his three hundred dollar suit. He greeted Boyle pleasantly, ordered Haig and water for them both, and led the way to a table in a window embrasure.

Boyle let a little of the whisky seep into his veins. "It's good of the old man to let me take up your time," he said. "Before you start, I must tell you I phoned Van Staden's office. He's incommunicado, contemplating The Collections."

"Someone put a button in the plate?" Lindsall had a voice that matched his face, quiet and silvery. "That will be the Paris Collections. Van Staden goes over every year to catch the big couturiers' previews. He reckons you have to watch the trend in clothes to keep ahead in the jewellery line."

"Does he keep ahead?"

"Oh yes. He's one of the top ten in New York City, and he has smaller boutiques in several other cities right across the States. He made his million way back."

"Legitimately?"

"So far as history relates. His old man saw Hitler coming just in time to ship Theo to relations in Vermont. They say he arrived with enough diamonds sewn into the lining of his coat to give him a start in life."

"Smuggling is legal?"

Lindsall grinned. "No. You have to tell what you've got. Theo's never been caught on the wrong foot, that I know of."

"Do you think he might have been involved in the Kostroma robbery?"

"No, wait, that was . . . how long ago? Thirty-nine? Uhm-uhm. The boy was only fifteen or so." Lindsall's pale eyes flickered, as if he was running through a mental index. "Round about then, I was with the F.B.I. We were told to watch out for certain receivers who might be buying in the Kostroma stuff, but nothing turned up. That was either an inside job, or top-flight professionals. I don't think Theo will throw much light on it. I just think he has the Midas touch."

Lindsall broke off to order sandwiches, rare beef, smoked salmon, and cream cheese with raisins. Over these, he gave Boyle a summary of Theo Van Staden's known activities; the type of work his firm undertook, his financial and business standing, his social status. He had married a woman of old Dutch stock, whose name was solid in Pennsylvania. They rented a luxurious apartment near Central Park, owned a place in Florida and another in Connecticut. Theo, in the material sense at least, had arrived.

Lindsall knew him, though not well. "He's a cold fish, no-one gets close to him. He's a great committee-man, though."

"So I note," said Boyle. "Mostly Anti. The Society for the Prevention of this and the Defence of that."

"He's the sort of character who's against most things. A Calvinist to the backbone. Energetic, hard, independent. Fond of isolation and great on the seven deadly virtues. He's not lovable. Not really good, I'd say. Know what I mean? That kind hunted witches in the old days. He's so damn proud and narrow and smug he feels entitled to stamp all over lesser breeds. You'll see what I mean, if you ever get to talk to him. I doubt if you will."

"Take you a bet," said Boyle. "Has Van Staden ever brushed with the law?"

"I told you," Lindsall clasped his hands and raised them before him, "the man is righteous."

"Yes." Boyle brushed crumbs from his jacket. "And that's often the sort that gets across the police. He protests about kids' parties in his neighbourhood, gets all steamed up about sinful nudity in the next-door pool, starts a whisper campaign against Jews or Catholics or Negroes. Bigots like that are hell on earth for the local authority."

"I'll ask around." Lindsall, like most good agency men, had informal ways of approaching a number of policemen. "I'd rather like to chip some of the white off that sepulchre, but frankly I don't have much confidence in my powers to do so."

"Any little incident will help. In the meantime, I'll keep trying to see him. I might take a run up to Connecticut, and see what they say about him there. I'm talking to his secretary at three, she may have something for me. Now let me fill you in on our side of the story."

He told Lindsall all he discreetly could about Emma Salt, and the Li Abas case. He also handed over a photograph of her in nursing uniform. He did not elaborate on the approaches she had made to the Villiers' family. This reticence was not lost on Lindsall, who said with a faint grin, "Mine not to reason why. I'll see what I can dig up in his apartment block, let you know if I hit blue clay. And if you move around, keep me posted."

They parted with goodwill. Boyle found a pay phone and telephoned Van Staden's secretary.

XXIX

THIS TIME, SHE greeted him with marked politeness. Boyle thought he also detected a note of chagrin. A watch-dog called to heel at the very moment of sinking her teeth into a juicy imported ankle.

Mr. Van Staden, she said, was sorry that he would not be able to undertake any business engagements until the end of the week. He had had flu, and his doctor prescribed rest and warmth. He was, however, interested in hearing any proposals coming from Villiers Glass, and hoped that on his return to New York he might make Mr. Boyle's acquaintance.

"So," concluded the secretary, "if you will suggest a time convenient on, say, Friday, I will be happy to make an appointment for you."

"That's very kind. The trouble is, I don't know if I will be in town. I leave tonight for Pittsburg and Cleveland. Safety glass, you know. I'm not sure how long the trip will take. If I might call you as soon as I'm able to confirm?"

"Certainly, Mr. Boyle."

"And that," thought Boyle as he replaced the receiver, "is a case of diamond cut diamond." He knew perfectly well that Van Staden would not dream of returning from vacation to bestow a private interview on a rep who arrived unheralded in New York. Nor did he see Van Staden as a second Eugène Thiers, interested in the quirks of human behaviour. It followed that Van Staden did not find Boyle's advent surprising, nor his request strange; an attitude in itself both surprising and strange. Theo the upright could have something on his conscience.

Back at his hotel, Boyle made arrangements for his trip to Connecticut. Theo Van Staden's house was a few miles beyond Guilford, at a place called Hollybrook, and the desk clerk confirmed that all main routes to that area were clear. For the minor roads he could not answer.

At a Drive-It-Yourself garage close by, Boyle hired a Volkswagen saloon which he judged would cope with all but deep snow. By four-thirty he was headed out of the city. He took the coastal road to New Haven, territory he knew quite well, and he made good time. But after that point he left the turnpike. The snowy convolutions of hill and valley confused him, and he was forced to drive more slowly. A truck-driver indicated a fatal short cut which cost him over an hour. By the time he made Hollybrook, the sky was jag-toothed with stars, the fences glittering with frost.

Boyle edged towards the centre of the little town. He passed a pretty green, a sprinkling of good colonial houses, but he was too tired and cold to appreciate them. He found a gas-station with a brightly-lit café attached, parked the car and walked into an atmosphere fuzzed with the smell of fat and coffee. Once he had downed a hot meal and three cups of coffee he felt almost human, and ready to think of his mission.

He introduced himself to the owner of the place, a long-jawed man who was quite prepared to exchange pleasantries. When Boyle mentioned the Van Stadens, however, he denied all knowledge of them with a speed that seemed suspect. Nor did any of the other people present offer any comments.

Boyle paid his check and left. As he reached the sidewalk a voice behind him said, "Mister? You're not going out to the Van Stadens' tonight?"

Boyle turned to study a thin young face, at once nervous and stubborn.

"No, I wasn't thinking of it."

"Because don't. They keep dogs." The boy moved forward into the lamplight. "I went out there one time, they nearly tore the pants off me. I mean, right there by the front gate, I wasn't trespassing or anything. I was just working on my subs. I have to get subscriptions for my list of journals. The top ten salesmen win a trip to Europe next summer. I thought I'd sell Mr. Van Staden something, all I got was a chewed-up leg. My dad made them pay, but after that I couldn't go back."

"Quite. Is that why they're unpopular? I noticed a certain coolness in there, when I spoke about them."

"They can make a lot of trouble. It's a small town."

Boyle nodded. After a moment he said, "Is there a motel or some place I can stay?"

"Yes, but if I were you I'd go to the Gooses." The boy grinned. "And I don't mean geese. They have a room free. A friend of mine boards with them, but he's on vacation in Maine." He gave directions for reaching the house. "You say Bob Turnwright sent you. You'll be okay there."

"Thank you. It's lucky we met." Boyle felt in a pocket. "I'd like to help with those subscriptions."

"No. No thanks, really."

"Then take my card. If ever you make London, look me up."

Boyle held out the card. The youngster glanced at it quickly, looked up at Boyle.

"An investigator?"

"I have no status in this country."

"But you're looking for her, aren't you?"

"Yes." Boyle heard the sharpness in his own voice. "Yes. Do you know about her?"

The boy took a step forward, but before he could answer a window swung open in a house across the street. A woman leaned out and shouted, "Bob?"

"Coming!"

"You come right now, I'm waiting for that butter."

"I'm coming." The boy's feet danced impatiently. He leaned towards Boyle. "You ask the Gooses, they'll tell you."

"Thanks, I will."

"'Bye!" The shouted farewell rang on the crisp air.

"Goodbye, Bob."

Boyle climbed back into his car with a sense of elation. Whatever the facts said, he was sure now that he had found the right Van Stadens. The wild goose chase, he thought with wry amusement, had led him to a golden Goose.

When the door of a house was opened to him five minutes later by a woman with white hair, sparkling red cheeks, and brilliant black eyes, he was almost ready to think he had found Mother Goose herself.

She made him welcome and led him into a living-room that couldn't have changed much over two centuries. Boyle saw a hearth flanked by baking-ovens, a settle draped with a patchwork quilt, a set of wooden chairs of a sparse and singular beauty. Involuntarily he smiled at his hostess and said, "You didn't by any chance shake your feather-bed out of your window, last week?"

She gave a rich chuckle. "No, no. Blame the weather men for the storms, not me. Samuel!" This last was yelled over an ample shoulder, and brought to the scene a man as round and shining as herself.

"Sam, this is Mr. Phillip Boyle, from London. He wants a room for a night or two."

"Yes?" A pair of shrewd eyes surveyed Boyle. "Some

kind of salesman, are you?"

"No." Boyle decided on the truth. "I have some enquiries to make for a client in Britain. I aim to see a Mr. Theo Van Staden, who I understand lives near here."

"Aimin' high." Mr. Goose ran a thoughtful finger along the back of a chair.

"So I'm told."

"Mr. Van Staden doesn't like strangers."

"And shows it?"

"He's not a mannerly person."

Boyle accepted this dictum in silence. Mr. Goose tilted his head and looked at him.

"And Bob Turnwright sent you?"

"Yes."

"Umh." Once more silence fell. Boyle stood it as long as he could and then cleared his throat. "That's a very beautiful set of chairs you have there, Mr. Goose."

"Shaker design." A sparkle reached his eyes, sun on a blueberry hedge. "It's not to everyone's taste. Too plain."

"A fine simplicity."

"You're partial to wood?"

"Don't know much about it. Porcelain's my hobby."

"Ah? Not easy to find that, these days. Too many dealers." Mr. Goose pointed a plump finger at the dresser on his left. "That plate, now. My wife's great-great-uncle brought it from China. I'll show you."

"Nothing of the sort." Mrs. Goose spoke briskly, as if she had concluded some unheard dialogue with her husband. "Mr. Boyle's not going to look at any plate that doesn't carry a bite of food."

"I've had my dinner, thank you kindly."

"Then a slice of raisin pie, and Sam will mix you a hot rum toddy. It's allowable, these cold nights, and the long way you've come."

Seated round the fire, the three attacked this supper with good appetite. The Gooses regaled Boyle with much local lore. From their talk he drew an awareness of New England, of a people determined to establish on any environment to which God called them certain standards of virtue and of comfort, a life both sturdy and graceful, deliberate and free.

He was entertained to find that they regarded the Van Stadens with something very close to pity. Indeed, Mrs. Goose said outright that she was sorry for Mrs. Van Staden. "She has no looks and no spunk. A woman needs one or the other. She's scared of her husband. You'd think she'd be able to hold her own. Her folks belong here and he doesn't. But she just kow-tows to him all the time. Frightened to open her mouth. They say he's got a wicked temper. Mind, I'll grant he had a bad time as a child. But a lot of folks had a worse time, and it taught them to value their own kith and kin. I don't take to a man who won't care for his own family, Mr. Boyle. Imagine, turning your own niece from your door?"

"Is that what he did?"

"Certainly is. She came up here about two-three years ago. Spoke to Mr. Jenner down at the post office. Told him she was Mr. Van Staden's niece and asked the way to his home. Wouldn't hire a cab and walked all the way out on her two flat feet, so we reckoned she wasn't blessed with the world's goods. And when she reached the house, Mr. Van Staden wouldn't even see her. I know it's true, because Lucy Applethwaite was helping Mrs. Van Staden in the kitchen that year, and Lucy heard the whole of it, although she didn't get a look at the girl."

Boyle pressed for more information without success. It appeared that few people had seen the itinerant niece even from a distance. Mr. Jenner of the post office, who had spoken to her, was no longer in Hollybrook, having been shifted to a job in Salem.

"No-one saw her leave this town," said Mrs. Goose, and the firelight made her shadow leap across the white wall behind her. "She just disappeared."

That night, as he climbed between sheets that smelled of thyme and lavender, Boyle reflected that the woman had come and gone like a figure in an ancient ballad, her image the more potent for the lack of a name.

He realised too the import of Mrs. Goose's sharp look, the tone in which she said, "she just disappeared."

Hollybrook believed Theo Van Staden to be capable of murder; not guilty of it, perhaps, but capable of it.

It was an interesting point.

XXX

THE VAN STADEN house was a shocking piece of architecture; literally shocking, thought Boyle, as he gazed at it from the crest of a neighbouring hill.

It stood in undulating country. Forests like fire and smoke converged upon a noble spur of land, and at the summit of this, where one hoped to find rubicund brick or weathered stone, there crouched an affront of grey cement, a ruthless glitter of glass.

The design had no joy in it, no hint of grace, nothing but a utilitarian ugliness. The windows were too prominent, the doors too deeply inset. The total effect was one of pop-eyed, toothless rage. Perhaps in summer that square and ordered garden might show some colour, but at the moment it was bare, the lower branches of the trees and shrubs pruned fiercely back, the grass clipped so that the skull of the earth shone through.

Boyle decided that house and garden had been arranged that way for security reasons. No-one could cross the lawns without being seen. The naked windows might declare that the owners had nothing to hide; but they also ensured that nothing outside should be hidden from them.

Round the entire perimeter ran a high wall topped with shards of broken bottles.

Boyle ran his car down into the valley and up the far slope, stopping at the point where the road converged on the Van Staden property. He alighted and walked a little distance in the shadow of the wall. After a short while his ears picked up a soft padding noise. Dogs, more than one, were pacing him. He checked, and made an experimental scrabbling against the wall. The padding stopped, but there was no growl. Boyle felt cold. Watchdogs that were trained to attack without sound could be classed as professionals.

Well, Theo Van Staden was a jeweller. There might be valuable stones on the premises. A man couldn't be run in for protecting his property.

Boyle went back to the car and drove round to the rear gates. The dogs were already waiting on the far side of the wrought-iron; a brace of German Shepherds with docked ears. One of them looked sane. The other swung its head in an arc, close to the ground, and its eyes had a crazed look.

Boyle stepped carefully up to the gates and peered through. Some distance away, a man was stabbing the turf with a sharp-pointed tool. He glanced up, saw Boyle at the gate, and walked slowly across to him. As he reached the dogs he said, "sit", and they obeyed him at once. He came to a halt and stared at Boyle without speaking.

"I wish," said Boyle cheerfully, "to talk to Mr. and Mrs. Van Staden."

"You can't." The voice was leaden, indifferent.

Boyle ignored it and went on, "I am passing through Hollybrook on a business trip. Mr. Van Staden has agreed to see me in New York, but it occurred to me that I might save him time and trouble by seeing him today. I'd be glad if you'd convey that message to him."

The man's shoulders lifted faintly. "No visitors."

Boyle reached into a pocket of his overcoat and took out his travel-wallet. No warmth of avarice showed in the man's eye. Boyle dismissed all thought of bribery, and instead selected two photographs, one of Emma Salt and the other of the facsimile Kostroma brooch. He found a business card and wrote on its reverse: "Emma Salt, also known as Emma Van Staden, proposes to sell the brooch to Adam Villiers. I am empowered to act for him."

He gave card and photos to the gardener, who took them without question and slouched off towards the house. The dogs sat like gargoyles and watched Boyle.

Ten minutes later the man returned, opened the gates and indicated with a jerk of the head that Boyle might enter. Boyle nipped back to his car, spun it smartly through the gates and accelerated up the drive. A glance in the driving-mirror showed him gardener and dogs loping behind. He circled the house, found the front porch and rang a peal on the bell.

A cheese-faced maid admitted him and led him along aseptic corridors. At various points they passed groups of antique furniture, French, English, and Early American. The pictures on the walls were modern abstracts. Everything was incredibly clean. Boyle felt he was walking through a private showroom, that every object was for sale. People might live here, but it was nobody's home.

At a turn in a passage, Van Staden himself appeared. He waited for Boyle to reach him, opened a door and waved the way into what was obviously a combined studio, work-room and reference library. There was a drawing-board, design table, a jeweller's bench, a number of optical instruments. The inner wall from floor to ceiling was hidden by books. And again, there was a rigid orderliness that hinted at the fanatic.

Boyle studied his host with interest. Theo Van Staden was a small man, spindle-shanked. His thin fair hair was combed sideways across the skull. His features were even; straight nose with wide-flaring nostrils, a small straight mouth like a split in the skin of a plum. He wore dark blue slacks, a dark blue Shetland wool jersey. He stood by the design table and the fingers of one hand, thick-tipped and long like the legs of a water-spider, rested on a pile of scale drawings. In the other hand he held Boyle's card.

"You changed your itinerary, Mr. Boyle?"

There was a very faint trace of Holland's accent in the flat Vermont delivery.

"That's right."

Van Staden picked up a pair of spectacles, put them on, studied the two photographs Boyle had sent in. After a while he laid them aside.

"I'm afraid I can't advise you about the brooch. I can't see why Mr. Villiers is approaching me."

"Do you recognise the woman in the photo?"

"No."

"Do you know anything at all about the woman calling herself Emma Salt or Emma Van Staden."

"Nothing whatever."

"There is reason to suppose that she has knowledge of your brother Alex, who died in Java during the war?"

"Knowledge? That is possible, I suppose."

"She may in fact be laying claim to your brother's name."

"That too is possible, though unjustifiable."

"Do you remember the Li Abas case?"

There was a pause. One spatulate finger lightly tapped the pursy mouth. "Yes, I recall it. When that case hit the headlines, police of various nationalities enquired whether the Van Stadens in the story were related to me. I was able to assure them they were not. My brother had no children. His wife was barren. Doctors in Holland were able to testify that she was unable to have a child. Naturally I would have been delighted to have positive evidence of my brother's fate, but it was not forthcoming."

"And Miss Salt has never approached you?"

"No." A flicker of apprehension darted across Van Staden's face.

Boyle noted it, but did not pursue the point immediately. He knew quite well that the jeweller was frightened; he would not otherwise have admitted Boyle to the house.

"Is that brooch in the photograph known to you, Mr. Van Staden?"

"It is familiar, but I'm afraid I can't place it."

"It is a facsimile of the Kostroma brooch, stolen from the family of that name in 1939."

"Indeed? I'm sorry, but I'm still not much wiser. At that time, I was only sixteen years old."

Boyle thought that this time the man was speaking the truth. Although Van Staden looked angry and perturbed, he also looked puzzled; as if his mind was running through old memories, seeking for illumination. If Emma Salt had approached him, then it seemed likely she had done so without mentioning the brooch.

Boyle spoke softly. "Two years ago, a young woman calling herself your niece came to Hollybrook and asked the way to this house. You refused to see her. Can you deny that she was the woman in that picture?"

An extraordinary change came over Van Staden's face. The

flesh paled visibly, the eyes became lightless. Boyle received a startling impression not of fear, but of hate.

"I saw no woman. I do not entertain blackmailers and thieves. My brother is dead."

"In that case . . ." Boyle rose to his feet and collected the photographs from the desk . . . "I'll say goodbye. Thank you for this little talk. Even a negative answer is informative." He smiled at Van Staden. "We have initiated enquiries about Miss Salt, both in Holland and in the Far East. Of course we will also trace her activities here in the States. If anything interesting turns up, we'll tell you."

Van Staden made no reply, nor did he accompany Boyle to the front door. Boyle made his way back through the house without difficulty. He half-expected to find the gardener and his dogs standing guard over his car, but there was no sign of life on the gravel drive-way. The gates at the far end were thrown wide.

Boyle drove for them like Orpheus for the gates of Hades.

XXXI

Boyle stayed long enough in Hollybrook to establish that nobody could identify the picture of Emma Salt. That did not worry him. Mr. Jenner in Salem would do the trick, no doubt; that was a matter of routine which Lindsall could deal with.

He parted from the Gooses with expressions of esteem and affection. Mr. Goose enjoined him to come again soon, and Mrs. Goose insisted on giving him a luncheon hamper that made the passenger seat sag.

He ate some part of this on the road south, and by mid-afternoon was back in New York, at Runyan's Agency. Lindsall greeted him affably.

"So how did you find the upright Van Stadens?"

"Upright, maybe, but not good." Boyle slid into the accent of Mr. Goose. "Y'know, Boston brown bread and a dose of salts can both be good for the parts, but I know which I'd rather swallow. There are some virtues that just seem to shrink the tongue, Mr. Boyle."

Lindsall laughed. He was evidently pleased with himself, and said jubilantly, "and I have news. Mr. Theo Van Staden had words with the police just two years ago. A resident of the block of apartments where he lives called in the law to stop a disturbance. It was claimed that Theo and a young woman were brawling in an upper foyer."

"Don't tell me," breathed Boyle, sinking into a chair.

"Yes, indeed. Sergeant Bellamy told me there was quite a rumpus. When he arrived, a lot of denizens of the lower floors had moved up to the twentieth to watch the fun. Theo was centre stage, with a young woman whose blouse was badly torn. This woman claimed she visited his apartment at his invitation and he attacked her.

"It was clear she'd given as good as she got. Theo had a black eye coming up, and his nose was bleeding on to his Charvet tie. He protested the woman was unknown to him, had entered his apartment by guile and trickery, had become abusive, and been ejected by him with the aid of his cook. The cook weighs about three tons and hails from the Bronx. She agreed she'd helped with the throwing-out, but she told Sergeant Bellamy that Van Staden argued with the woman for over an hour before the fight started. Bellamy felt the cook had enjoyed the whole shindig and was inclined to sympathise with the young woman rather than with her own employer.

"He also felt . . . and this is interesting . . . that the young woman was getting a kick out of the situation. The other residents were kind of watching Van Staden from the corner of their eyes, and it seemed as if it might be time to move the drama to some place else, such as the police station.

"But at this point, the woman stepped forward and made a speech. She said that she didn't want to press any charge. She intimated that although Theo was a nasty character possessed of nameless faults, he was a married man and there was no call to upset his blameless wife. The whole encounter was a case of mistaken intent, and it would be best if everyone went home and forgot it. She apologised gracefully to the tenants for disturbing their peace, and to the cook for various

124

physical damages. Without ever saying anything actionable, she discredited Theo in the eyes of his neighbours and his cook. Bellamy says it was all he could do to keep from applauding.

"He made up his mind to let it go at that. Van Staden plainly didn't want to take the matter further. Bellamy read the crowd a short lecture on the inadvisability of wasting the time of officers of the law; and left. He remembers the whole incident with great clarity. He was much struck by the personality of the girl, describes her as 'a tall, dark doll, with eyes that made you feel kinda brainwashed'. Bellamy isn't an impressionable cop. If he says the girl's a spell-binder, it's probably true."

"And this, of course," said Boyle, "was Emma Salt?"

"Well, this is another interesting point. Bellamy filed a routine report, which gives the girl's name as Abbess. L-e-e A-b-b-e-s-s."

"Then," said Boyle triumphantly, "that definitely ties her in to the Li Abas case. It also makes a deliberate liar out of Van Staden. I showed him a picture of Emma Salt and he said he'd never met her."

"That could be merely an attempt to avoid further trouble," suggested Lindsall. "He may well have been telling the truth when he said his family were not the Van Stadens concerned in the Li Abas case. The girl can easily be a confidence trickster, set on making a false claim to the Van Staden name. If that's so, then Theo is entitled to throw her out of his house, and to try to hang on to some privacy."

"I think," said Boyle, "I shall put a call through to Hollybrook and let Theo know we know about the fight in the foyer."

Lindsall pushed a telephone forward. "He'll rush screaming for his lawyers."

This opinion proved to be right. Theo Van Staden heard Boyle out in silence, and then said in tones straight off the Tundra: "Now, you hear me, Mr. Boyle, I don't discuss important matters with underlings. Your principal is Adam Villiers. You may inform him that I shall shortly be in London, and at that time I shall make it my business to call on him and convey to him the advice of my lawyers. Until then I have nothing to say to anyone on this subject. Good day."

The line clicked. Lindsall, who had been listening on an extension, grinned broadly.

"Flushed him."

"It looks like it." Boyle squinted at the clock on the wall. "And now I must see about getting back to London myself. It looks as if the eagles are beginning to gather."

XXXII

ADAM WAS AT this time in Amsterdam, in the office of Inspector of Police, Pieter Loots. This man was affable and slow-voiced. He had rosy cheeks and a double crown that made his grey hair stand up in schoolboy tufts. His English was good, and showed little accent.

"I am afraid," he said, raising bland blue eyes to Adam, "that I do not quite understand your interest in the Li Abas case, Mr. Villiers."

Adam said carefully, "I'm compiling a history."

"I see. You know the case was officially closed many years ago?"

"So I understand. You were on it, Inspector?"

"Yes. I worked for three years to try to establish the identity of the Van Stadens who handed over the child. I failed. The case was closed."

"And you're satisfied with that decision?"

Loots spread thick fingers. "That is not significant."

"I am interested," said Adam, "in a certain Mr. G. J. Van Staden, deceased."

"Oh?"

"I have just come from Berne in Switzerland, where I attempted to interview a Mrs. Gebhardt who was once Mina Van Staden."

Loots smiled bleakly. "She refused to see you?"

"Yes."

"I could have saved you the trip, Mr. Villiers. She was always a very difficult person to interview."

"I have an agent in New York at the moment, trying to talk to Theo Van Staden."

"I doubt if you'll get much out of him, either."

"In other words, Inspector, your department is convinced that these are not the Van Stadens concerned in the affair of Li Abas?"

Loots shrugged. "The family was considered. There was a son Alex, left Holland just before the Nazis came. We were able to establish that Alex Van Staden and his wife flew from Amsterdam to the Far East in April 1940. We know also that they were childless. Mrs. Van Staden could have no children. She had a ... what do you call it, everything removed ..."

"Total hysterectomy?"

"That is right, thank you. The child in the Li Abas case must have been born before the time of that flight, and they had no such child. It follows they could not have given their child to Li Abas."

"Could someone have impersonated them, taken their place on the flight? Someone who did have a child?"

"It is not very likely. And where did the real Alex and his wife go, then?" Loots' smile was benign, but his eyes were watchful. It seemed to Adam that the policeman was almost hoping to be challenged.

Adam said, "And the brooch found in the possession of Li Abas; that was a copy of the Kostroma sunburst, wasn't it?"

Loots sat perfectly still. "How did you know this?"

"My lawyer was out in Java for many years. He knows the case."

"Indeed?"

"Can you tell me why there was no publicity given to that aspect?"

"I can. By the time the Li Abas case broke, we knew the answer to the Kostroma robbery."

"And that is?"

"That there was no robbery."

As Adam stared, the Inspector's eyes lost some of their coldness. "The Kostroma family, the French branch, was always very extravagant. Especially the old baroness. She had been selling the original stones for years, and wearing copies. Then the war came. The jewels were insured by a firm with Vichy sympathies. She was a patriot. She was also in money difficulties. She decided to defraud the insurers. She arranged for her collection of fakes to be stolen. Her chauffeur drove the truck which vanished at the Swiss border. Luckily, the baroness was never able to complete her plan and claim the insurance. The Nazis invaded France. She got away to Switzerland, where she died before the end of the war. She left instructions with her confessor that the police must be told the truth. Of course, the case could not be dropped just like that, but we knew we need not look for the Kostroma jewels."

"What about the fakes, what happened to them?"

"Some of them she sold in Zurich, to people who didn't ask questions. Anyone could have bought the fake Kostroma sunburst, Mr. Villiers."

"None of this was reported in the Press."

"We don't tell the Press everything. There are sometimes reasons one must not. We did not wish to hurt the Kostroma family by printing the story. Two of the sons died well in the war. The third son was in a position of international importance. What good to prove the old baroness made a mistake, that she was almost but not quite a crook?" Loots picked up an ashtray and placed it neatly at one corner of his blotter. "So you see, there was no link to be shown between the Van Stadens and the Kostroma sunburst. No link between the Van Stadens and Li Abas. Policemen need evidence before they can act."

"I understand." Adam, looking at the cherubic countenance before him, thought he did. "Luckily, I'm free to think what I like. I've certain theories. I can't discuss them at the moment, but if ever I come close to proving them, I'll let you know."

"That will be a favour, Mr. Villiers."

"I'd like to ask one thing. Can you give me the address of G. J. Van Staden's wife?"

"She is no use to you. She's in a mental hospital."

"Where?"

Loots sighed. "We have already asked so many questions, Mr. Villiers. You will just be spitting in the lake. But if you insist, it is an expensive private hospital at Amandel. That is near Delft. You can get there by coach or car, there is a travel agent one block up the street, on your right."

He wrote something on a piece of paper which he passed across the desk. "When you get to the hospital, ask to speak to Dr. Rom. Mention my name."

"Thank you very much indeed, I'll do that."

When Adam had shaken hands and departed, a long thin officer appeared in a side doorway of Loots' office.

"It's you who should be in that asylum. They told you to lay off the Van Stadens, didn't they?"

"So I have. If Mr. Villiers wants to nose about, I can't stop him."

"Think he's got a new angle?"

"Have to wait and see, won't we?"

Out in the street, a steady drizzle smoked above the roof-tops. Adam turned up the collar of his overcoat, glanced around to get his bearings, and headed for the travel agency.

XXXIII

AMANDEL PROVED TO be a charming small town, the sort of retreat where a number of well-to-do folk have succeeded in beating off the threat of industrial encroachment. Managers and executives were thick on the ground, but the nearest factory site was seven miles away.

There was a good deal of bright water shining between the leafless trees. The houses were new and gay, or old and burnished. Their brick, tile and whitewash, rosy in the winter sun-set, seemed a living testimony to the Dutch virtues of good husbandry and good living.

The hospital stood on the outskirts of the town, secure in the acres of a home farm. Adam was shown at once to Dr. Rom's office, and given sherry and freshly-baked sugary cakes. Dr. Rom came in fifteen minutes later, a youngish fifty with wise thick-lidded eyes and a soft voice. When Adam had explained the purpose of his visit, to satisfy his mind that the family of G. J. Van Staden was not concerned in the case of Li Abas, Dr. Rom turned down his mouth and sighed.

"Are you a journalist, Mr. Villiers?"

"No. I have a personal interest in the matter."

"In what way?"

Adam sensed that Rom was in his way as adamant as Loots. Where the Inspector was concerned with the truth of an answer, Rom was concerned with the validity of the question. He would not regard even the gratification of the social conscience as a reason for disturbing the peace of one of his patients.

Adam reached within himself and produced a plea that surprised him.

"I've been approached by someone who may be the child concerned in the Li Abas affair. I feel I must make certain enquiries. You can say it's a matter of conscience."

Rom nodded. "The child is possibly the only person who has any right to re-open a very painful investigation. Have you told the police about her?"

"No."

"I see. I must tell you at once, don't hope for new evidence from anyone at this hospital. The enquiries have been exhaustive."

"I thought you might let me talk to Mrs. Van Staden."

"There would be no point. The arterial degeneration is such that there is no coherent thought left. There is nothing there for you to talk to."

"You mean she's just a vegetable?"

"She's a human being who is deprived of the physical mechanism for intelligent thought. Perhaps she has some obscure pilgrimage to complete, but we can't share the journey, in the ordinary way."

"Then how could it hurt to let me see her?"

"She still feels, she is still aware. She understands when she is in hands of love, and she is capable of fear and distress. I won't let you see her because it might cause her suffering. She can't help you, you must take my word."

"I do, of course." Adam watched Rom light a cigarette.

"But tell me what you can about her, will you?"

"When the war ended, she was rescued from a Nazi camp. Her husband was dead, her family scattered, two sons gone, her own health broken. When the Li Abas case happened, the police questioned her about her son Alex. It was then that the disorientation of her mind became evident. She was childish, afraid, no confidence could be placed in her statement. At last they left her in peace."

"How long has she been here?"

"Eight years. When the mental distress became very marked, she was difficult in the home, her family committed her to Amandel."

"So they make generous provision?"

Rom's mouth tightened. "They can afford it."

"You don't like them?"

"My feelings do not concern you, I think."

"They might. You can't know."

"Very well. You can say, to me a member of a family is a member for life. I can see no excuse for putting the old into institutions before there is need."

"You think Mrs. Van Staden could have been happier outside?"

"She did not impose much on her relations. They are very rich. The son is in America. The daughter gave her mother the use of a cottage on her property in Berne. A gardener's cottage. She liked that. She was always fond of flowers."

"She lived alone?"

Rom shrugged. "The daughter was close. I believe they set her old ayah to care for Mrs. Van Staden."

Adam studied his host. "They could have committed her to a place less comfortable than this; less expensive?"

"Possibly. There are State hospitals."

"At least, then, they fulfill their financial obligations to her?"

"Oh yes." Rom's thick lids drooped, he moved the cigarette a little so that the smoke broke into a thin riffle. "They do that."

There was something in the quietness of his voice, some force, some anger, that told Adam that he had touched a vital issue. He leaned forward to ask another question, but as he spoke, Rom looked up and shook his head.

"I can't discuss my clients with you, Mr. Villiers. Tell me, have you anywhere to stay in Amandel?"

"Not yet, but I can easily find . . ."

"Nonsense. You must please stay with us. Quite all right if you can put up with four little boys and their noise. My house is just across the square. I'll take you there now. You've had a long day, you must be ready for a drink and a hot meal."

XXXIV

NOTHING COULD HAVE been kinder than the Rom's hospitality, nothing more normal than their home. Yet that very kindness and normality made Adam intensely aware that across the courtyard in the complex of the hospital, were people whose illness set them cruelly apart, in a distorted and abnormal existence.

He slept badly that night. Long before it was light he was wakened by the distant whine of a factory hooter. He lay for some time hoping to drop off, but decided at last to get up and walk round the home farm.

He dressed and made his way out of the house. Someone was already moving about the kitchen. Away to his right, the low frieze of Amandel was pricked with lights; and the lands between shone with a tremendous effusion of blue, pearl and copper-red.

Adam took a path that led past cowsheds and pigstys to the river. He skirted that for a mile or two until his way was barred by a canal where a dozen children in red and blue siren-suits were busy skating. He stood watching them until the cold began to bite, and then turned south again towards the hospital.

By this time it was full morning. Adam had made a complete circuit of the buildings, and as he approached the main square the sun glinted on polished glass and fresh paint. He realised suddenly that this was truly an asylum, a place where the sick took refuge not in blind pity, but in the knowledge and skill of men like Rom.

As he stood there, a bus appeared on the road from Amandel.

A number of people alighted; a man in blue overalls with a load of parcels, two nursing sisters, a plump couple bickering like starlings, an elderly Eurasian in a white widow's sari, a red-faced cleric. Most of them set off at once towards the central block of buildings, but the woman in white turned aside and made for Rom's house. As Adam watched, the front door opened and Rom ran down the steps. He approached the woman, took her arm and turned her away. They hurried in the direction of the hospital. Once they both glanced up and back, and it seemed to Adam that they were looking at his bedroom window.

He waited until they were out of sight, and then re-entered the house by the kitchen door. Mrs. Rom pounced on him, and made him sit down to a gargantuan breakfast. They were soon joined by Rom and the boys, the conversation became as loud and erratic as was natural, and there was no chance to tax Rom with further questions.

Nor did Adam believe that these would be of any use. Rom had said all he intended to say.

At nine o'clock, the doctor and his wife accompanied Adam to the bus. They waved away his thanks, and Rom said, "I only wish I could help you more." Adam thought he meant it.

The bus drew away, swung north-west from Amandel, across flat and water-seamed country.

Adam surveyed the prospect from his window. Someone, was it Mrs. Rom, had told him Mrs. Van Staden had been born near here. In spring there'd be fields of flowers. Now the earth was dark and barren. Strange how a landscape coloured the people who sprang from it. Was that why they so often returned in old age to the place of their birth? Dust to dust, ashes to ashes.

A thought struck him, and he reached into his pocket for the folding map given him by the Amsterdam travel bureau. Spreading it open on his knees, he searched for a name.

Rijswijk? That was it.

He found the dot on the coastline not far from Delft. It should be possible to reach there by late afternoon. There'd be time to look at the records; with luck one might even find the priest.

XXXV

In England a thaw had set in, the first salivation of Spring's hunger. The warmer air thrust along the Thames Valley a thick stink of mud and machine-oil, fish batter, wet grass and detergent. On the south face of Glass House the cleaners sprawled and swung, leaving in their wake a blue brilliance. Twenty floors up, in his office, Matt Kinsman glanced at a slip of paper, pulled a telephone towards him and dialled Grace's extension. Getting no answer from the penthouse, he tried Adam's number. Grace answered.

"Hullo, love," said Matt. "I wanted to ask you, what's this about a Board meeting on the 14th?"

"Wally wants it."

"Two weeks early?"

"He says it's advisable."

"But why? Grace, you've noticed the date, two days after we're due to meet Miss Salt?"

"Yes. I don't think that means anything." There was a pause, then Grace said flatly, "And don't worry about Wally. I can handle him."

"He's in an odd mood. I wouldn't be too sure of him, if I were you."

"Leave him to me."

Matt, replacing his receiver, shook his head.

Wally Kepple addressed his secretary, a dark clever young man with a constant smile. "Have you the list of responses for the 14th?"

"Here, sir."

Kepple glanced down the acceptances and refusals. The secretary said, "Not good. Putting it forward, we've cut out

134

the busiest men. That means some of the best. I'm afraid those present will be mostly the lightweights."

Kepple nodded. "Can't be helped." Secretly, he thought, all to the good. Lightweights were easier to stampede.

Grace sat at Adam's desk, a folio of drawings open in front of her. She leaned forward, pressed a switch on the intercom box.

"Jessie? Come in here, please."

Miss Fergusson appeared. Grace tapped the folder. "These Flamingo drawings won't do. I told Koch I wanted a complete rethink of form and decoration. This is simply a rehash, the Gilda shape over again. That was a flop in 1961 and it won't take now. Send the whole lot back to Koch and ask him to do as he's told . . . politely, of course."

Jessie, bending to pick up the folder, looked worried. "They aren't Koch's drawings, Mrs. Villiers."

"I can see that quite plainly. They're Mrs. Corelli's and they will not do. Koch is in charge of table glass and I want his work, no-one else's."

"Mrs. Corelli has already started the scale extensions."

"Then she will have to scrap them. All right, Jess, if it frightens you so much I'll tell her myself. But get these back to Koch."

Alone again, Grace stood up, pressing her fingers into the aching muscles of her neck. She felt a thousand years old. Damn Zoe for working up a departmental thing at this time. Her childish jealousy of Koch would have to be checked at once, before it drove him crazy enough to resign.

Grace moved slowly about the room. There was so much that was urgent, and she felt only this lethargy. Nothing seemed to matter much except Adam, his love and respect; and in a short while, a few days, that would probably be gone.

She picked up a shallow dish from a side-table. Pale grey, opaque, it had been the prototype for the Nimbus line. Hers and Henry's. She pressed the glass against her forehead, touched it to her cheek, felt its coolness through her closed eyelids.

There had been so much in those days; Henry, the child, the great empire of Villiers Glass, adventure and innovation, travel and famous names, success in society and success in business. Most of it was over. Three realities remained, Adam, the Company, the approach of death. There could not be much time left for any of them; and no time, no time at all, for anything else.

XXXVI

AT SIX O'CLOCK the same afternoon, Walter Kepple left his office and went up to his apartment. He took a shower, dressed in slacks and pullover, poured himself a glass of Amontillado and carried it to the huge window that overlooked the river. It was a purely reflex movement. His eyes took no note of the intricate mosaic of London. Blind, self-absorbed, he sipped his sherry. From time to time a tremor shook his body, there was a tension about him that came strangely close to pleasure. He was waiting for a turning-point in his life, for the telephone to ring.

He had known from the moment he spoke to Emma Salt that she was one of those beings who have the power to precipitate crisis, who wherever they go break down the ordinary patterns of society and create tumult and change.

Alone of all the people in Glass House, Kepple understood the nature of that force. He could match it with an animal dynamism of his own. In another age, he would certainly have hired assassins to deal with the woman. As it was, he intended a destruction no less total, albeit bloodless.

At the same time, he knew she provided him with opportunity. He had watched her invade the minds of those close to him, he had seen how she isolated each from the other. Isolation weakened them. It strengthened Kepple. He was used to working alone. Emma Salt had levelled the odds for him.

Another thing she had done. She had turned his love into his enemy. She had turned Grace against him, and so set him free. For ten years he had set only one limit on his ambition, the need to consider Grace. Now he need admit no check.

He could take whatever he wanted; and what he wanted, what he would take when the moment arrived, was the Villiers Glass Company.

At ten minutes to seven the telephone rang. Kepple went over to it without haste, picked up the receiver gently.

"Kepple speaking."

"This is Phillip Boyle. I have the address."

"One moment." Kepple reached for a message pad. "Yes?"

"Suite three, Fennell's Hotel. Just off Knightsbridge. He's signed in as Hugo Kriel."

"Thank you, that's very satisfactory. That ends your assignment, Boyle. You can get some rest, I expect you need it."

"Yes. When does Mr. Villiers get back, Mr. Kepple?"

"Tomorrow morning, the early plane. I'll give him a full report."

"I'll be round myself to see him, sir."

"As you like."

"Goodnight, Mr. Kepple."

"Goodnight."

Kepple replaced the receiver and stood staring down at his hands, braced like a pianist's on the rim of the table. He lifted them, brought them down in a sharp, triumphant chord. Crossing to the cloakroom, he jerked an overcoat from a hook, checked his pockets for keys and cash. He shrugged into the coat, switched off the lights and let himself out of the front door. He ran down the stairs to the floor below, walked past the lightless porch of Adam's flat and stopped at Zoe's entrance. He put out a finger and pressed the bell, smiling to himself.

She was a long time coming, and then did not at once open the door. He could hear her moving in the hall, peering at him no doubt through the seeing-eye device. He said in a soft voice, "Hurry up, Zoe."

"Who is it?"

"You know damn well who it is."

She unlatched the door but left it on the chain. Her face, puffy and petulant, leaned towards the crack. She smelled of stale flowers and whisky.

"What do you want?"

"To talk."

"I'm tired, Wally, I've just got in."

Kepple's hand shot forward and grasped her wrist. "Sober up. Theo Van Staden is in London. Do you understand?"

For a moment she stared at him owlishly. Her lips moved and the pupils of her eyes contracted sharply. Kepple let go of her arm. "Open up."

She obeyed him, releasing the chain. He followed her into the drawing-room. She was wearing a kaftan of magenta wool, and the patent leather shoes that matched it lay on the floor near the sofa. Next to them was a blue folder of drawings. Kepple probed it with a toe.

"You should have let Koch do the work in the first place, my sweet."

"You shut your teeth." She was already reaching for the decanter on the side table, but Kepple came up behind her and caught her by the shoulders, spinning her round to face him.

"You're not drinking any more while I'm here." He deliberately tightened his grip, drawing her forwards and upwards so that she was forced to meet his eyes. "You are going to tell me all about Van Staden."

"I don't know him!"

Kepple suddenly slackened his grip. Zoe dropped backwards on to the sofa. He stooped and picked up the folder, tossed it into her lap.

"You know what that means, Zoe? It means that Koch is in and you are out. One year from now, he will be Director of Design."

"We'll see about that."

"Indeed we will. Don't count on Grace for help. She isn't President of the Company now. You haven't many friends left on the Board, and Adam thinks you're old-fashioned. How fatal that sounds, doesn't it? You could afford to be crude, a bad draughtsman, short on experience with glass. Like Koch. But old-fashioned, no. Koch has ideas, Zoe, and you have none. Koch has energy and drive, you are old and tired. He is beginning, and you are finished. Some time quite soon, the move will start to push you out and promote Koch. All that

138

stands between you and oblivion is Walter Kepple."

Kepple bent towards her, bright-eyed. He saw the slackness of her muscles, the thread of saliva in one corner of her mouth. He felt no pity for her, no more than she had felt for him through ten years of hunger and humiliation; but she was valuable to him. He did not want her to crack now. He sat down on the sofa and took her hand.

"All right, Zoe, perhaps I can help you. But first you will have to tell me about Theo Van Staden." As she started to speak, he shook his head. "No, don't waste time lying. You know what I mean. Yesterday morning Phillip Boyle returned from the States. He came to Glass House to report to Adam. He talked to me, and told me that he believed Van Staden would visit England in the near future. He was more right than he knew. An hour later, we received notice from an agency in New York that Van Staden was booked on a flight arriving here this afternoon. I instructed Boyle to arrange for a man to meet the plane and find out where Van Staden is staying. That has been done.

"You understand, Zoe, what this implies? It means that Van Staden sets the utmost importance on Emma Salt. She is important enough to warrant a journey across the Atlantic. If he wants to see Adam, that means he wishes to take joint action against her. He knows something about her, something vital. I have to know what he knows."

Zoe watched him with a sliding, sideways gaze. "I don't know anything about him, I've never met him."

"My dear," Kepple patted her hand, "when someone is blackmailing you, as I am, you really must pay attention to what he says. You are going to tell me about Theo Van Staden, and in return I will do my best to ensure that Koch does not get your job."

She said in a whisper, "Grace?"

"Grace will not hear about this."

"I can't. I can't remember."

Kepple leaned across her and took up the decanter. He poured whisky into two glasses, gave one to her. He leaned back in his own corner of the sofa. His face, his thick curling hair, might have been carved of stone. He was a pagan god, relentless, empty-eyed. After a moment he said, "Tell me about the cards. Henry's index cards. You drew them for him?"

"Yes."

"You drew number 183? The brooch?"

"I can't remember. It's too long ago."

"Don't lie."

"I'm not lying! I drew a lot of cards, I don't remember what they looked like!"

"Where were they kept?"

"I think with Henry's private papers. I suppose when he died the Company took them. But a few years ago, Grace moved them. It was when we came to Glass House. She moved them up to the penthouse."

"And Emma Salt found them. How many were stolen?"

"Grace says, five."

"And one of them was the card we found on Christmas night?"

"I tell you I can't say that. I'm not going to put myself on the spot, just saying what you want me to. I don't remember, that's all."

Kepple took a pull at his whisky. "All right, leave it at that. Tell me about Henry. The week Henry died. You and Grace went down to Norfolk. You tidied up the house, you packed up the silver and china and glass. What about the ornaments and jewellery?"

"What d'you mean?"

"Did you see the brooch? Did Lisbet have it?"

Zoe's face became blank and Kepple leaned closer to her. "Soon, Zoe dear, you won't have this excellent whisky provided by the Company. You won't have this flat, you won't have your car. Those are Company property, they'll go to Koch. Oh well, you've had thirty good years, perhaps it's time you were cut down to size. There'll be plenty of people in Glass House glad to see that happen. I've often wondered how you managed to stay in a place where so many colleagues loathe the sight of you. It certainly wasn't talent that endeared you to Grace. What then? Something you knew about her? Something you learned that week in Norfolk after Henry died? And now it seems that Emma Salt knows as much as you do. In a little while, we'll all know. Your advantage is purely momentary. So what do you gain by keeping your trap shut? Tell me now, and when the cold winds start to blow, at least you will have my love to keep you warm."

Zoe huddled her shoulders as if she already felt the bite of that winter. She said dully, "How do I know you can do anything?"

"You have no guarantee. My promise isn't worth much, but it's better than nothing." He smiled, and his words fell as gently as snowflakes on a grave. "Did Lisbet have the brooch? No? Can you be sure? What did she take when she left? Think about Lisbet, Zoe. Remember. Tell me about Lisbet."

It was over an hour later that Kepple left Zoe's flat. He took the lift down through the dark levels of Glass House to the crystal glitter of the foyer. He stood there for a minute or two, gazing about him with secretive, exultant eyes. Then he walked through the arcade to the private enclosure at the back of the building, where his car was parked.

As he drove out of the rear gates and turned left to take the river road, an ancient Riley pulled from the kerb some distance behind him. Kepple was too uplifted, too absorbed in his plans, to notice that he was being followed.

XXXVII

ADAM HAD PLANNED to catch the airport bus to the terminal; so he was surprised, when he came through the customs, to find Phillip Boyle waiting for him in the reception area. The agent came thrusting through the crowd with unusual impatience.

" Morning, Mr. Villiers. Good trip?"

"I slept. I spent most of last night frigging around in a bloody cold town called Rijswijk. Lisbet Jonkers' place of birth. What brings you here?"

"Mr. Kinsman asked me to come down. He wanted you to know at once, Theo Van Staden is in London."

"Really? Looks as if we hit blue clay."

"Seems so." Boyle was already headed for the exit, leading the way to where his Opel Rekord was parked. As they climbed into the car, he said, "I want one thing clear, Mr. Villiers. When I agreed to take this job, I signed on with you in your personal capacity. I'm not working for the Villiers Company, I'm working for you."

"That's never been in doubt, surely?"

"Apparently it has. Last night, Mr. Kepple tried to call me off the job."

"Then I hope you disregarded his orders."

"I did, and just as well." Boyle slid the car into the thickening skein of city-bound traffic. "But I'll give you my report in the proper order, if you don't mind." He began to recount the events of his sojourn in the States, speaking quickly and precisely. In conclusion, he said, "the main fact is that Emma Salt has already approached Van Staden, and attempted to pass herself off as his niece. You'll note that at that time he kept quiet, obviously hoping the thing would blow over. Now here he is in London. So either he believes her claim is justified, or he knows it comes close enough to the mark to call for joint action with you."

Boyle paused, and Adam saw that he was choosing his words with care.

"It's hard to put this without offence, Mr. Villiers; but the inference is Mr. Van Staden hopes to do a deal with you. Else he wouldn't be here. The second inference is Van Staden knows that Emma Salt has a claim on you as well as on him. Else he wouldn't hope for any help from you."

Adam was silent for a moment, and then said, "I think that's true, yes."

"In which case," Boyle drew a deep breath, "I think it's my duty to tell you that Mr. Kepple approached Mr. Van Staden privately last night. If he tells you about it himself, well and good. If he doesn't . . . you're warned, sir."

"What happened?"

"Two days ago, when I arrived back from the States, I went to Glass House to see you. You weren't back, and Mr. Kepple said I must make my report to him. I gave him some of the facts, not all. It was a difficult situation, I didn't want to antagonise Mr. Kepple, in all the circumstances."

"No, I understand."

"When Lindsall of Runyan's agency tipped us off about Van Staden's flight, Mr. Kepple ordered me to meet the plane, and find out where Van Staden was staying. Of course I couldn't do the job myself, Van Staden knows me by sight; but I put two good men on to it. Last night, at ten to seven, I phoned Mr. Kepple and gave him the name of Van Staden's hotel. He thanked me and tried to tell me the job was over, I could go home and forget all about it. It occurred to me that Mr. Kepple might be planning to talk to Mr. Van Staden. I kept both men on duty. At ten thirty-five I was informed that Kepple and Van Staden were together in a restaurant called The Dim View. My chaps couldn't get close enough to overhear the conversation, but it was plain it was a business conference. After an hour Van Staden went back to Fennell's Hotel, and Kepple to Glass House."

"You told Mr. Kinsman about this?"

"I spoke to him on the telephone, about midnight. He asked me to come down and meet you this morning. He's staying at Glass House, with Mr. Kepple. I'm not telling you all this because I want to make trouble, sir, but it's the second time Mr. Kepple's tried to direct the investigation to suit his own book, and I don't like it. I'm employed by you, and I don't double-cross my clients."

"Thank you. One more thing, did you tell my mother about Van Staden's being in London?"

"I didn't, but she knows. She telephoned to ask me if it was true."

"Did she discuss it with you?"

"No. I said he was here, and Mrs. Villiers just thanked me and that was all."

They were being sucked into the metropolitan maelstrom. Adam saw the translucent pinnacle of Glass House flash against the lowering sky, and for the first time it moved him with a strong and possessive pride. He came close to understanding his mother, who had created it, and Kepple, who coveted it.

He said, "about Rijswijk. . . ."

"Yes?"

"It's where Lisbet Jonkers was born."

Boyle nodded. "I know, but her family moved away when she was ten, to Delft."

"They went back after the war. I had a hunch about it. I remembered Matt told me Lisbet came of coast people, that she loved sailing and the sea. It struck me her folks might feel the same, and might have gone back to Rijswijk when they retired."

"You traced them?"

"No, they're both dead, but I found an old parish priest who knew them. They did retire to their old home town. The priest told me quite a bit about them. Honest, God-fearing people, he said. He knew Lisbet as a child, too. Said she was weak and greedy, but fond of her family. He knew about her collaboration with the Nazis, and was very sad about it, not only from the patriotic angle, but because it kept her from coming to see her parents. Apparently when she returned from England she sent them quite big sums of money, which they wouldn't accept. They turned it over to the church."

"Didn't want collabo money, I suppose."

"But it wasn't collabo money at that stage. It was perfectly respectable, her inheritance from my father, in fact."

Boyle frowned. "It doesn't make sense. If it was honest money, why wouldn't they accept it? You mean they knew even at that time that Lisbet was dishonest?"

Adam gazed ahead of him with an oddly twisted smile. "No. I'm beginning to think that Lisbet Jonkers was an honest woman. That's why she was afraid to go home."

XXXVIII

WHEN THEY REACHED Glass House, Adam went straight to the penthouse. He found Grace already dressed, sitting over an electric fire in her study. A small table stood beside her, laden with papers which she was sorting. As he approached, she turned with a smile and put out her hand.

"Well, darling?"

He took her fingers. They were cold and light. She looked terribly ill, there was a bluish glow about her skin. All the time he had been in Holland, he had planned what he must say to her. The closer he came to the truth, the more urgent it was to speak frankly. He had known the interview would be difficult. She would fight to dominate events as she always had in the past. He had intended to be as obdurate as she.

Now he saw that he had reckoned without her illness. Her mind might still be immune to argument and shock; her body certainly was not.

He said gently, "Mother, you know that things are moving rather fast? Theo Van Staden has come to London."

"So I hear." Her eyes smiled up at him, as calm and reassuring as if he were six years old. "I'm not worried about him."

"I came to tell you that I'm going to invite him to the meeting tomorrow night."

Grace raised her eyebrows, and inclined her head as if she were giving thought to Van Staden for the first time. "Well, you may be right. If the man has something to say, perhaps he'd better say it to all of us. He can help us put the woman in her place and then we can forget her."

"My dear," Adam could not keep the concern from his voice, "you do realise that things can't be hushed up any longer? If Emma Salt means anything, she means to expose the facts. It won't be pleasant for us."

"Of course it won't. But we must keep a proper sense of values, mustn't we? The work of years, the love of years, isn't undone by a single malicious act. You'll find we'll deal with the creature quite quickly. The unpleasantness will pass. Everything will be as it was before."

He shook his head.

"Wait and see," she insisted, and gave his hand a final pat. "Leave it to me, Adam. Don't worry."

She turned back to her documents. Adam watched her for a moment and then said, "Very well. I must go, I've things to do."

"Good, dear." She spoke over her shoulder. "Try and get some sleep. We must be at our best tomorrow."

Adam left her and went to his own office. He summoned Matt Kinsman and Wally Kepple and told them of his interviews in Holland. They discussed the arrival of Van Staden. Adam waited for Wally to mention his approach to the jeweller, but nothing was said.

At noon Kepple returned to his accounts. Matt lingered for a while.

"Got any ideas, Adam?"

"One or two. If you don't mind, I'll keep them to myself for the present. I don't want the issues prejudged. I want things to take their natural course tomorrow night."

"As you like." Matt tugged at his lip. "Watch Kepple though, he's going to make his play soon."

"I know. I'm glad. I want a showdown. If I'm to be President, I don't want it on his sufferance."

"I hope you're sure of your ground."

"Reasonably."

"Well. I'm on your side, right or wrong. I'm too old to be impartial."

"Thanks, Matt."

Later Adam called Halstead from the Legal Department and conferred with him for over two hours. At the end of that time Halstead looked extremely worried.

"You understand, Adam, that I can't give you a snap decision on the legal questions involved? We'll have to go into those very carefully. I don't know of any precedent. I trust that if you ever have further facts at your disposal, you'll confide in me at once?"

"That I promise."

"You don't feel I should be present tomorrow night?"

"No. For one thing it would inhibit discussion. For another, if I take my lawyer along, Van Staden will demand his, and I'd rather keep this within the family circle."

"I hope you are able to do so."

"I'll try not to involve the Company."

Halstead sighed. "It may be a problem to decide where the

Villiers family ends and the Villiers Company begins."

It was now three o'clock. Adam gave a few instructions to Jessie Fergusson, and then went up to his apartment. He raided the kitchen, found bread and ham and pickled walnuts and ate them standing. He made a pot of coffee and carried it through to the living-room.

He spent the rest of the afternoon and evening drawing up a complete report of his time in Holland. He left out no details, however trivial they seemed.

When the draft was finished, he dictated it on to a dictaphone. He then carried the dictaphone over to the Hi-Fi recorder near the window, and made a second taped copy. This he sealed in a box, and addressed to Matthew Kinsman.

By this time he had reached that point of weariness when sleep seems impossible. He moved about the apartment, going over arguments in his mind. At last he stepped out on to the terrace that overlooked the river.

The wind had sharpened from the east.

On the face of Glass House, the platforms left by the cleaners surged like boats on a heavy swell. Far down in the street, people moved, battling head down against the wind. They did not seem part of a crowd. They were solitary figures, each one engaged in a hand-to-hand fight against the elements.

Perpetual loneliness, perpetual struggle, was that the pattern of life? It held good for the people in Glass House. Matt, Zoe, Walter, his mother, each was close at hand and each was trapped in a separate existence, a final reticence. Was it because they faced, as he did, the truth about Emma Salt? No doubt each was busy with the material implications of that truth; the effect it might have upon fixed property and the extent to which it could disrupt a comfortable existence.

And yet he was sure that this was the least of the challenge of Emma Salt. When first he had seen her walk across the parking-ground, he had felt an affinity for her. He had known she concerned him. Ultimately, her life and his must meet and reach some just accommodation.

Perpetual struggle, perpetual loneliness, that had been her experience. His too, surely; a constant effort to preserve his mind intact, an endless search for an answer to the question "who am I?"

That was it. The truth about Emma Salt was also the truth about Adam Villiers. When he defined her limits, he would define his own. That was a fact of life, probably the only one worth noting, that each time one encountered a human being, one came face to face with oneself.

He went inside; locked the dictaphone and the extra tape in his desk; and just contrived to undress and fall into bed before he was asleep.

XXXIX

AT SEVEN-THIRTY ON January 12th, while Grace Villiers was still at the dinner-table, the telephone rang in the hall. She went out to answer it.

"Grace?" Matt's voice was exasperated. "I'm bringing Zoe upstairs at once. She's half-lit already."

"What? Oh how maddening. I kept her with me until six o'clock."

"She's made up for lost time."

"Bring her, then."

Grace went through to the kitchen and collected the coffee percolator, set it with seven cups on a tray, added brown sugar and cream-jug. She told the cook to hurry with the washing-up.

"Get home as soon as you can, Elsa. It looks as if it's going to storm."

"It does, ma'am. Blowing a gale already. Be a nasty night."

Back in the drawing-room, Grace placed the coffee tray on a table near the hearth. She glanced about. Sofa and chairs waited in a half-moon, the temperature was right, the lamps lit and the curtains drawn.

Going to be a nasty night.

She stooped and plugged in the percolator. The water boiled, darkened, sank and rose. She heard the elevator coming up and soon Matt appeared, holding Zoe by the arm.

Zoe was a draggled wasp. She thrust past Grace with an

uncertain step, slumped into the nearest chair. When Grace took her a cup of black coffee, she pushed it aside so that the liquid slopped into the saucer. "I don't want that muck. I'm sick of the lot of you." Her beady gaze wavered. "I feel sick. Grace, I feel. . . ."

"Come." Grace lifted her and pulled her out to the cloak-room, held her head while she vomited into the lavatory bowl. When the spasm was over, she washed Zoe's face, dabbed cologne on her temples.

"What made you be so silly?"

Zoe whimpered. "I'm frightened."

"Who frightened you?"

But Zoe merely shook her head.

When they returned to the drawing-room, Wally had arrived and was talking to Matt. Grace went straight over to them. Her hand closed round Wally's wrist.

"What set Zoe off?"

Kepple glanced at Zoe and shrugged. "She's all right."

"Did you say anything to her, Wally?"

But Kepple gestured towards the hall. "They're here." Adam was crossing towards them, accompanied by a skinny man with the skittering gait of a water-spider.

"Mother, this is Mr. Theo Van Staden, of New York."

Grace held out her hand, smiling. "How do you do? It was kind of you to come."

"My pleasure, Mrs. Villiers." Van Staden's voice conveyed a curious mingling of dislike and deference. His restless eyes flickered from face to face, the fingers of his left hand slowly straightened and curled in a furtive movement. "My father was acquainted with your husband, I believe."

"They were friends and business associates."

Kepple spoke. "Eight o'clock. If Miss Salt is punctual. . . ."

"She will be," answered Van Staden, and once more his eyes went swiftly round the room.

Matt caught the look. "It's not bugged."

"Today, one can't be too careful." The jeweller fingered his tie. "Nothing is sacred."

Grace pointed towards the hall. "Adam, please?"

Over the lift, the indicator glowed. The gilt doors opened.

Emma Salt stepped out.

She wore black, a plain black coat which she handed to Adam as he approached her, a black dress of very simple cut. Her dark hair was wrapped smoothly together at the back of her head, and she wore little make-up.

The sombre guise did not subdue her outlandish effect. Like the brooch pinned to her left shoulder she burned with an inward fire that was almost virulent.

She moved slowly forward, checked just inside the drawing-room and faced the assembly.

"Let me introduce you." Adam drew her towards Grace. "My mother. And this is Walter Kepple, Financial Director of Villiers Glass, whom you have met. Mr. Theo Van Staden. Mrs. Zoe Corelli, our Director of Design. Matthew Kinsman, Director of Production." He turned back to the woman at his side. "And you? Which of your titles do you prefer to use?"

She inclined her head at an angle of indifference. "That's for you to decide. Emma Salt, Emma Van Staden, I answer to both. But if you want to get the party going, why don't you try something new? Call me Emma Villiers."

XL

"VILLIERS?"

Matt's startled roar sounded the louder because no-one else shared his surprise. He swung round to Adam.

"What the bloody hell does she mean?"

"We'd better all sit down," said Adam, "and let her tell us." He took the chair on the far right of the crescent, and motioned to Emma to sit next to him. Slowly the others took their places. Like tigers in the ring, they watched Emma, the tamer and controller, the person they would most like to tear apart.

She faced them placidly. Her hands lay quiet in her lap.

"It seems," she said, with a half-smiling glance, "that of all my names, Villiers is the one you like the least; so let's deal with it first. My claim to it comes from this." She touched the brooch that winked against the dark fabric of her dress.

"The Kostroma replica. It was made by Henry and Lisbet Villiers. After the Kostroma collection disappeared, the family didn't need the copy. They were pretty broke. Henry Villiers bought it from them cheap, and gave it to Lisbet. It came to me from her."

"How?" said Matt sharply, and she answered him calmly, "By inheritance. I am the legitimate child of Lisbet and Henry Villiers."

"That is the first lie," said Grace.

"It is true," corrected Emma, "as you very well know, Mrs. Villiers."

"No, now wait." Matt's great hand reached out and tapped the arm of Emma's chair. "Let's have it straight. You've come here to claim that there was a child born posthumously to Henry and Lisbet Villiers?"

"Yes." Emma's nod was almost kindly. "I was born in Amsterdam on January 12th, 1940. The birth was entered as illegitimate, but that was not true. I can establish that the Lisbet Hermanus Jonkers recorded as my mother was the same Lisbet who married Henry Villiers."

Zoe's voice cut in waveringly, "January 12th? That's tonight."

"Yes." Emma's dark eyes glinted. "Welcome to my birthday party, Mrs. Corelli."

"Anyone could find out the date." Zoe swayed forward. "Look up the records, invent some story. Anyone could do that."

"I am the daughter of Henry and Lisbet."

Zoe was on her feet, moving towards Emma as if hypnotised. "That's not true. You don't look like anyone I know. Not like Henry, not like Lisbet."

"I resemble my maternal grandmother, Katerina Jonkers."

"And will she come forward to speak for you?"

"She's dead."

"How very convenient!"

"People remember her. There are pictures of her."

"Hah! People will remember anything if you pay them enough."

"Zoe," said Grace sharply, "please sit down."

"I'll do what I damn well please!" Zoe whirled round and almost lost her balance.

"You're being a nuisance."

"Nuisance, yes, is that all you think of me? Nuisance, old bore, finished, is that it?" Zoe's voice was soaring towards hysteria, and Matt stood up abruptly and put an arm round her shoulders.

"All right, lass. Sit down now. Come and sit here, next to me. Umh? That's right."

She let him lower her to a chair. Her fingers gripped the sleeve of his coat. "I thought she was dead. Matt? They told me she was dead."

"Take it easy."

"She can't come back from the dead." Zoe's head turned confusedly towards Emma. "Why'd you have to come back?"

"I have a right to live."

"Not here. Not here."

"We'll see."

Matt said heavily, "Grace, did Lisbet have a child?"

"Not to my knowledge."

"Did you suspect she was pregnant at Henry's death?"

"I didn't take any interest in her condition. I owed her nothing. She was well able to look after herself."

"That's strange," said Emma. "You've always claimed she was such a fool. Couldn't do a thing right, isn't that what you told people? Didn't you say you had to go down to Norfolk and fix things up after my father died?"

"When my husband died," said Grace with bitter emphasis, "I went down to see that he was given a decent funeral. Lisbet would have made a profit on that if she could, buried him in deal and charged for oak, she had a peasant's greed. Do you think I'd have left her to dispose of my husband's property, his house and land?"

"Why do you speak of him as your husband? Your marriage was over."

"It was blessed by the church. It ended when Henry died, not before."

"Ah, yes, you wanted to believe that, didn't you? You told yourself that Lisbet didn't matter, that she was just nothing. You told yourself Henry would come back to you. How did you feel when you found out Lisbet was going to have his child? The dream was a bit thin, wasn't it? Lisbet's child was going to grow up in England, be recognised by the law, by all the people you cared about. It was going to have Henry's name and Henry's money, and it was going to put paid to the legend of Grace Villiers. Is that why you shipped my mother back to Holland?"

"She went of her own will, not mine."

"You took her back. You took her even though you knew the war was coming. You found her a flat and settled her in it. Three months later you went and visited her again, to make sure she was doing as she was told. You went back a third time when the baby was born. Don't lie, Mrs. Villiers, I can prove you made those journeys."

"Certainly you can prove I visited Holland. I frequently did so, on business. I did not see Lisbet, however, and you will not prove I did."

"You saw her, and you saw the child. Strange, isn't it? You were one of the first people to see me. I've often thought about it. How did it feel? Why didn't you just hold a pillow over my face? It would have been quicker and kinder than what you did to me."

"Kinder." Zoe's voice bubbled up foolishly. "That's right. Grace said it was kinder to the child."

"Be quiet!" Grace's head snapped round. "You are not drunk, Zoe, so don't pretend you are. Who put you up to this?"

"It's true, Grace, that's what you said, kinder to the child."

Grace started to speak, but Adam silenced her with a gesture. "Zoe," he said, "when did you learn that Lisbet was pregnant?"

Zoe mumbled, "She told me."

"Who?"

"Lisbet. After Henry died. We were all there in the house together. Lisbet wanted to go home. She cried all the time. She looked ill. I asked her straight out if she was pregnant, and she said she was."

"You told my mother?"

"Of course." Zoe's eyes went slyly to Grace. "But I didn't tell anyone else."

"You didn't inform my father's lawyers?"

Zoe shrugged. "Darling old Adam, Lisbet wasn't my worry. She wanted to go home and she went."

"She didn't go back to Rijswijk."

"Well, she disappeared off to Holland. I never heard another thing about her. I supposed she'd got rid of the baby. She didn't want it. She said so."

"Didn't you think of the inheritance problem?"

Zoe made no answer, and Adam insisted quietly, "Any legitimate child of my father was due to inherit a considerable fortune. After the payment of death duties, the estate stood at one hundred and thirty thousand pounds. That was not the money that Morgan Villiers tied up in the Company, but my father's personal estate. Under the terms of his will, my mother received twenty-five thousand pounds outright. She already held a large portion of the Company's shares, and at the time of the divorce Henry had given her the London house with all its furnishings and fittings, and also a car and valuable jewellery."

"I made the money that bought those things," said Grace, and Adam nodded.

"No doubt. My father provided generously for you, that's what I'm saying. He also provided for Lisbet. He knew she was foolish about money, and he tried to give her security. He left her a steady income from shares worth twenty-five thousand pounds, to be held in trust during her lifetime. He knew that at that time the shares were very low, because the Company was going through a bad time; but he also knew that they were bound to appreciate once the wartime contracts began to pay off. On Lisbet's death, the trust was to be wound up, the shares to revert to the estate."

"What provision did he make for you, may I ask?" Van Staden's damp skin gleamed as he bent forward from the shadows.

"The bulk of his estate, after provision had been made for my mother and Lisbet and certain charities, was left in a second trust, to be administered for the benefit of his legiti-

154

mate issue. The value of that trust was some seventy thousand pounds, invested in Villiers Glass and its subsidiaries. As my father foresaw, when the war came Villiers shares climbed sharply, and by the time the trust matured, that is when I turned twenty-five, its value was well over two hundred thousand pounds. And of course there's been further appreciation during the years since that date."

"All the money came to you?" said Van Staden.

"Yes."

"Because," said Emma, and her smile flickered like the tongue of a whip over the tigers in the lamplight, "Adam Villiers was held to be the sole legitimate issue of Henry Villiers. In other words, when Mrs. Grace Villiers concealed the fact that a daughter had been born to Lisbet Villiers, she did her own son a very good turn indeed."

Matt lifted his head. "You're accusing Mrs. Villiers of deliberate deception. I warn you, you'd best watch your tongue when you speak before witnesses."

"Tell me this, then. Why didn't she speak to the lawyers? Why didn't she tell them about the child's birth?"

"We've only your word for it that Grace knew of the birth. And I'd like to remind you it was Lisbet who concealed the fact of birth, not Grace. It's up to the mother to see that the child is registered. And why didn't Lisbet write to the lawyers herself? Everyone says she was so money mad. If there was a child, it was due to inherit thirty-five thousand at the age of twenty-five. All Lisbet had to do was wait."

"She wasn't one to wait that long. She wanted ready cash and plenty of it. Grace showed her how to get it. When she went back to Holland, she was allowed to take what she wanted from Norfolk. She took a car, furniture, silver. When she died a few years later, she had nothing. She'd sold the lot. She traded security for the sweet life, and it was damn nice business for your friend Grace."

Grace, who had risen and moved to stand near the hearth, now turned and faced the circle.

"There was no question of fraud," she said. "Life isn't that simple. Money isn't that simple. You didn't know Lisbet."

She raised one hand and lightly touched her forehead. They

saw in her face a deeply puzzled look.

"I knew her. You know the woman who takes your husband from you. You think about her all the time. I knew Lisbet was vain, greedy, feckless. I knew from the start she wouldn't keep the baby. I was afraid she might have an abortion. I warned her of the risks. She told me then she meant to give it away to anyone who wanted it . . . except me, of course. I tried to explain to her how I felt. It was Henry's child she was carrying. I couldn't stand by and see her . . . let a child of his be given away like a pound of cheese. I offered to adopt it. Lisbet refused point blank. She had her own jealousies. She hated me quite as much as I hated her. She didn't mean to care for her baby, but she was determined I shouldn't have it.

"But you can put it right out of your head, Miss Salt, that Lisbet's child was tricked out of a share of Henry's money. Lisbet knew the facts. She acted of her own free will. She placed the child in adoption, and under British law a child so placed forfeits the right to inherit from its natural parents."

"She didn't place the child, you did." Emma Salt leaned forward and the brooch sent out a shaft of light that shone on her cheek like a claw-mark. "You got rid of that baby without scandal, without risking your own neck, and you kept hold of the Villiers money. There was no need to arrange any adoption. Lisbet Jonkers had parents, decent folk who would have cared for her baby. They never even knew she was pregnant. Why?"

"Because," said Grace wearily, "Lisbet refused to tell them. She was legally married, the child was legitimate. The Jonkers would have regarded it as a great wickedness for her to abandon it. They would have plagued her with moralities. She wouldn't even go home, in case they found out about her pregnancy."

"You could have told them the truth."

"What right had I to interfere?"

"You had a duty to the child. You had a duty to see my own people kept me! You cheated me out of my family!"

"Nobody can force a woman to keep a child she doesn't want. Lisbet had made up her mind to give her brat away. I couldn't influence her. I had no power to interfere."

Emma broke into laughter. "No power? You? You couldn't interfere so far as to tell my own grandparents that I existed, but you could set up an adoption. You couldn't influence Lisbet to keep her brat, but you could con that brat out of thirty-five thousand pounds. You had the whole thing planned from the beginning. You fixed it for Lisbet to sell her child, and the price was a car, some furniture, and a smart flat in Amsterdam. It was a good trade you did there, Mrs. Villiers. You lost a few things that meant nothing to you. Lisbet's child was disinherited, which meant a gain to your own son of thirty-five thousand. And that sum's more than trebled in the past quarter of a century. Adam's worth a lot of money, and he's ploughed back plenty into Villiers Glass. There isn't one of you in this room who hasn't done all right out of Lisbet Jonkers' brat."

"I beg to point out," the voice from the corner spoke with cold precision, "that that remark does not apply to me. Neither I nor any member of my family profited in any way."

Emma moved back to her own place, sat down and regarded Van Staden with flat contempt.

"When you say 'profit', Theo, of course you mean money. I know that humanity doesn't count for much with the Van Stadens. But they did get something out of the deal, didn't they? A baby isn't a bonus you pick up every day of the week."

"None of this can be of any value to you, Miss Salt."

"Not too fast, please. You accept the fact that Lisbet Villiers gave birth to a legitimate daughter on January 12th, 1940?"

"Oh yes, I accept that."

"And do you agree that that child was placed with prospective adopters, through the agency of Grace Villiers?"

"I agree."

"Is it not a fact that those adopters were Alex Van Staden and his wife Susannah?"

"You may say so if you like."

"Very well. Let us forget about Emma Villiers. Let us consider the case for Emma Van Staden."

XLI

Matt Kinsman broke the silence. "You say that Mrs. Grace Villiers arranged the adoption. What evidence can you produce to support that assertion?"

"The evidence of Mr. Theo Van Staden."

Matt glanced enquiringly at the jeweller, whose right hand moved in a gesture of acquiescence.

"Yes, I am prepared to testify that Mrs. Grace Villiers oversaw the arrangements for the adoption of the child."

Grace went over to the sofa and sat down. She folded her hands on her knee and said, "Mr. Van Staden, until tonight, I never saw you in my life."

"You did not see me. I saw you. I can testify to that. You were the third party who acted as intermediary in the adoption of Lisbet's child. I think it's time we all spoke plainly. I'm a businessman and I want this sordid affair settled once for all. These are the facts as I know them. In February 1940 I saw Mrs. Grace Villiers for the first time. I was fifteen years old, the youngest member of my family. Mrs. Villiers came to our home in Amsterdam to see my elder brother Alex and his wife Susannah. They were at that time home on long leave from Java. I chanced to overhear them discussing the visit of some person they seemed to think was important. They were whispering in corners, very secretive. I thought at first it must be politics they were discussing. The war was close. I made it my business to keep an eye on them. On the evening in question I kept a specially close watch."

"Once a snooper," said Emma, "always a snooper." Van Staden threw her a venomous look.

"I observed carefully, that night. I saw Mrs. Grace Villiers walk up the alley at the rear of the house. She was met in the hall by my brother Alex, who conducted her upstairs to the small salon. There he and Susannah talked with her for a long time. I was unable to overhear much of what was said."

"Keyhole blocked?" said Emma.

"It is as well for the cause of truth," said Van Staden, "that

I heard enough to establish that Mrs. Grace Villiers had come to the house to discuss with my brother the legal adoption of a child born to Lisbet Villiers. A girl child. I had often heard of Mrs. Villiers, of course, since her Company and my father's were associated through business. I saw Mrs. Villiers occasionally in after years. There was no doubt about her identity. Nor is there any doubt that in late February a child about five weeks old was placed in the care of my brother and his wife. Their intention was to adopt this child."

Matt Kinsman said, "If that was their intention, then there can be no question . . ."

. . . "Wait." Theo held up a hand. "The story does not end there. On April 2nd, 1940, my brother was directed by his firm to leave Holland, which was about to be invaded. He was instructed to return to Java. You will recall the unsettled and dangerous times. Alex and Susannah did not wish to leave the child in Amsterdam. They obtained the consent of Mrs. Lisbet Villiers to take the baby with them. They intended at some later date to make the adoption legally secure. But as you know, the war engulfed them. The Japanese entered hostilities, Java fell. My brother and his wife, and the child with them, vanished into limbo. After the war, we were unable to establish with certainty what happened to them. They did not survive the war, that is sure."

"I survived," said Emma, almost to herself. "I lived with Li Abas. I survived. I am alive, Theo."

"Very much alive." Theo's pale eyes surveyed her. "Very much alive to the chance of perpetrating a fraud." He glanced round the circle. "Two years ago, this woman came to me in the States and tried to suggest that she was the child of Lisbet Villiers, the child given to my brother Alex. She claimed me as a relation. I soon formed the opinion that she was a criminal and an opportunist. She had the insolence to invade my household at Christmas time. It seems to be a habit with her. No doubt she thought the holy season might further her ends. People are sentimental at that time of year. Her arrival was a great shock to me and my wife. It revived old griefs. We had buried our dead but she sought to revive them. She was without mercy."

"You wanted them dead," said Emma. "You wanted me dead. After the war, when the refugee organisations tried to trace my family, you never said anything. You never admitted your brother took a child. You kept quiet, you and your family. You could have helped Li Abas if you'd spoken, but you kept quiet. Li Abas hanged himself while you did nothing."

"She came to us," said Theo, quickly licking his lips and glancing about him, "because she hoped to secure a fortune. My family has wealth and a certain social status. She planned to fleece us."

"I didn't want your damn money."

"Do you expect us to believe that? Do you really expect all these sensible, responsible people here tonight to believe your sudden urge to meet us had nothing to do with the fact that we're all rather rich? Oh come, Miss Salt!"

"You know I asked for nothing."

"I didn't give you the chance. I knew what you were after, the moment I set eyes on you."

Emma was silent for a moment, then said in a low voice, "When I came to you, I thought I was coming home."

"Oh now, that's very pretty! You see, my friends, how this woman plays upon our most sacred sentiments? Let me tell you she's taken good care to arm herself with facts as well. Spent years getting us documented. She knows my worth to the last dime, I'll be bound."

"I came," repeated Emma, "because I needed to talk to you. I accepted the past, the death of your brother, the death of Li Abas. But don't you understand, I needed an identity? I'm a displaced person. I don't know who I am. When I was sixteen I started looking for my own people. You're right, I spent years looking for facts. When I was ready, I came to see you. I was fool enough to think you'd want to see me, and hear what I had to say. I didn't expect to prove much. I thought I'd tell you about myself, you'd listen, and we'd talk. There was no sentiment in it, Mr. Van Staden, and I didn't want anything from you. But you wouldn't even talk to me. In Connecticut you turned me away from the door without seeing me. In New York you treated me like a thief."

"I told you then, as I am telling you now, you have no legal claim on me or mine. You are not my brother's child. You see, Miss Salt, there are only two ways in which such a relationship can be established. The one is by birth and the other is by legal adoption. You claim that you are by birth the child of Lisbet and Henry Villiers. You may or may not be able to prove that. I don't know and I don't care. What you cannot prove is that you were legally adopted by my brother and his wife. No legal adoption was ever concluded. No documents were signed, no process of law enacted. Therefore the position of my family is quite clear. You have no lawful status as Emma Van Staden, and you can make no claim of kinship with us."

Van Staden nodded round with brisk assurance. "I make this point in the presence of you all. This woman is not legally entitled to associate herself with my name. Whether she has any claim to yours, Mrs. Villiers, is not my problem. However, I agree that in certain circumstances your interests march with mine. If Miss Salt continues to try and prove she is Emma Villiers, my family may well be dragged into it. There may be unwholesome publicity. That is why I decided to come to London to talk frankly with all you good people. I have already had a very constructive talk with Mr. Kepple, and I think I can say we reached solidarity on all important matters."

He turned back to Emma. "I am not a hard man, I do not want to be unchristian towards you. The temptations may have been great. But I want to tell you that if you take this matter to court, you will be crucified. I advise you to listen very carefully to what Mr. Kepple will have to tell you, after which I am sure you will see that it is best to go home and forget what was never more than a foolish dream. I am speaking for your own good. Mr. Kepple? Perhaps you'd like to take it from there?"

And Van Staden, with the modest air of a man who has spoken with discretion and with generosity, leaned comfortably back in his chair.

XLII

"THANK YOU."

Kepple came to his feet, smiling.

"It is important, I feel, to take the heat out of this discussion. We must forget sentiment and get down to facts. I have talked to Mr. Van Staden. In my opinion, it is a pity that two years ago he reacted to Miss Salt in a rather emotional way. Feelings were aroused which can't easily be soothed. Miss Salt's resentment has led her to take up an attitude that helps neither herself nor us. What we need is a rational approach to a very unfortunate situation.

"Let's state the prime fact first; Miss Salt is determined to establish her true identity. Ladies and gentlemen, we may not be able to tell her who she is; but in my belief we can tell her quite plainly who she is not. Mr. Van Staden has told us she is not Emma Van Staden. He bases his case on the fact that although his brother took a child, no legal adoption was ever concluded. Miss Salt, do you contest that argument?"

Emma stared at him without speaking, and Kepple gave a brisk nod. "I see you don't. Then we come to the other facts at our disposal. We will accept, for the moment, that Lisbet Villiers bore a legitimate female child. We also accept that Mrs. Grace Villiers, acting as she thought in the best interests of the child, tried to arrange for its legal adoption by Alex and Susannah Van Staden. Proof must be forthcoming, but let us agree that the daughter of Lisbet was, in February 1940, at the age of five weeks, placed with the Van Stadens.

"Now. We move to the other aspect. Seven years later, in Java, a man named Li Abas turns up as custodian of a girl child and a replica of the Kostroma brooch. There follows the drama which is now common cause.

"Miss Salt claims that she is the child of the Li Abas story. No doubt it will be possible to show that she was indeed cared for by him, transferred to the Salts and thence to an Institution.

"There are thus two areas in which theory is capable of factual proof. Those two areas we can remove from the present debate. We accept that Lisbet Villiers placed her child with Alex Van Staden and his wife. We accept that a couple named Van Staden, not necessarily Alex and his wife, placed a child and a brooch with Li Abas.

"What we do not accept, I think, is that those two children were one and the same person. That, I assure you, is the crux of the matter. In any adoption, the identification of the child is a prime concern. What proof have we that this young woman sitting here tonight is the same child born to Lisbet Villiers? None at all. Not a vestige."

Emma Salt touched the brooch on her breast. "This is proof," she said.

"Explain," answered Kepple with a patient look.

"Certainly. My father, Henry Villiers, made the brooch. He gave it to his wife Lisbet. After his death she took it to Holland, and it passed from her to the Van Stadens, with the child."

"And why should Lisbet, a woman notoriously mercenary, part with a piece of jewellery worth a couple of hundred pounds?"

"It wasn't worth a groat to her," said Emma. "By the time she reached Holland, the Kostroma jewels had been stolen. The police were on the lookout for the pieces in the collection. Lisbet knew if she wore the brooch, or tried to flog it, someone might spot it and start asking questions; and that was just what she couldn't afford. Any trouble, and people would know she was pregnant. Her parents would come down on her, and Henry's lawyers. The only people who might buy the brooch were the Alex Van Stadens. She sold it to them."

"Can you prove that?"

Emma shrugged and Kepple's teeth glinted. "Of course you can't. It's mere invention. No, Miss Salt, there is no evidence that the Alex Van Stadens received the replica from Lisbet; and without that vital link, you can't show that it was Lisbet's child with Li Abas. You have no connecting link. Your chain breaks down; in fact, no chain can be shown to have existed.

"Let me conjure up another picture for you. Van Staden

is a common enough name in Holland. Let us imagine that a couple named Van Staden, unknown to any of us, a couple with one baby daughter, happened to be in Switzerland in 1940. As Adam has learned from the Amsterdam police, at that time the Kostroma collection, consisting of fakes, crossed into Switzerland. Old Countess Kostroma, a political refugee in Zurich, sold the pieces for what she could get. The brooch went to this Mr. and Mrs. Van Staden. They, like so many Dutch citizens, went out to the East Indies, where they were engulfed by the Japanese invasion. They met up with Li Abas, handed their child to him, and offered the brooch as payment. They were captured by the Japanese and died in some camp. Isn't that theory at least as acceptable as yours, Miss Salt?"

Emma's face was flushed. "I'm not interested in theories, Mr. Kepple. Only in the truth. My father made that replica. He made Zoe Corelli draw an index card for it. That card was in his files. I found it there."

"And stole it?" said Kepple with a triumphant thrust of the hand. "You tricked your way into the home of Mrs. Grace Villiers; and are you going to stand up in public and admit that while you were there you made a search through her private possessions? That you found the card and removed it with several others? The Nursing Council will take a serious view of your very unprofessional conduct."

"I don't give a damn what anyone says about me."

"Perhaps you'll give a damn when I say I don't believe for a moment you found that card in the index. None of us believes it. Mrs. Corelli will tell you she never drew such a card. Mrs. Villiers will confirm that until Christmas Night she had never seen or heard of the drawing. It won't take a court of law long to decide that you have tried to pull one of the oldest confidence tricks in the world.

"You were brought up in an Institution. I've no doubt life was hard for you, and you came to realise that you had only one useful asset, the replica brooch. When you were sixteen years old, you began to investigate the circumstances of your own past. You made patient, exhaustive enquiries, travelling all round the world to do so. Somewhere along the line you obtained a list of all those people named Van Staden whom the police had questioned during the Li Abas case. You checked on them, probed their past histories. You found that one family of Van Stadens, living in Amsterdam, had in 1940 taken into their care a baby girl. You set yourself to check through the records of births in Amsterdam for that period. In time you turned up the name of Lisbet Jonkers. There was a good deal of information on the police files about her, because she'd been a collaborator during the war. You found that she had been married to Henry Villiers, and had worked with him on the manufacture of costume jewellery.

"And there, Miss Salt, you saw the way to make an easy fortune. You came to England, wormed your way into the good books of Dr. Fraser, who is doctor to Grace Villiers. Through him you gained access, as a nurse, to this penthouse. You found the set of index cards drawn by Mrs. Corelli. You took careful copies of her drawings and the italic script she used. You also stole five of the cards. Four you no doubt kept. The fifth, number 183, you destroyed, replacing it with a fake card showing the Kostroma brooch. That fake card you planted in the foyer downstairs on Christmas Night, trusting that we would fall into the trap of believing it had come from Henry's index. Once that card was held to be genuine, then there was a good chance that you could establish a thread of evidence that would show that the Kostroma replica indeed passed from Henry to Lisbet, from Lisbet to the Van Stadens, and from them to Li Abas. You manufactured evidence, Miss Salt, and we came very close to swallowing it whole."

"That card is genuine. It can be tested any way you like."

"It will be." Kepple turned to Grace and laid a hand on her shoulder. "My dear, you need have no fears. All Miss Salt can produce is a spurious card and a string of clever lies. There is no legal case for us to answer."

Emma spoke sharply. "Time will tell. Your word against mine, and I have the evidence. See you in court, Mr. Kepple."

He swung back to her. "I warn you, don't try me too far. I've made allowance for your past misfortunes. I realise they may well have affected your mind. But I won't allow this

165

to go any further. If you try to cause trouble, I won't scruple to see you crucified."

"I won't be alone." Emma's dark eyes rested on Grace.

"Don't imagine you can harm Mrs. Villiers. Her family, and the Van Staden family, are wealthy and influential. They will fight you with all their resources. The legal costs alone will ruin you."

"Perhaps my costs will be guaranteed."

"I see. You're thinking of the gutter press, no doubt. I suppose you could find a newspaper that will guarantee costs provided you give them sole rights to your story? But the gutter press, my dear, tends to taint its beneficiaries with gutter slime. You'll emerge from all this without a profession, without money, and certainly without a reputation."

"Oh, Kepple, but I'm used to that. I don't need a profession. I've got enough money, and I don't care a jot what people think of me. Can your girl-friend say the same? She's going to show up as the trickster who sold her husband's child, and let his widow die in Nazi Europe. What will her reputation be worth, would you say?"

"You won't be allowed to publish libels against Mrs. Villiers."

"I'll take her to court, and the case will be reported in the press. All I have to do is tell the truth, and let people decide for themselves which of us smells the sweeter."

She began to rise. Adam leaned over and caught her wrist. "One moment, Emma."

She shook her head. "There's no more to say."

"There you're wrong. Give me a moment? Please?"

She hesitated, then relaxed back in her chair. Adam turned to study the faces pale in the lamplight. "There's one aspect we haven't considered," he said. "To me, it's the most important."

"Well," Kepple moved impatiently, "what's that?"

"The possibility that Miss Salt is speaking the truth. What concerns me, Wally, is whether her claim is justified. I want to know if Emma is my half-sister."

XLIII

"MY DEAR ADAM," Kepple took a pace forward, "surely I've made it plain that no answer to that question carries any weight unless it's given by a court of law?"

"Ultimately, it must so be given." Adam met Kepple's opaque and angry gaze. "What bothers me, Wally, is how we approach the point of legal decision. We came here tonight to meet Miss Salt, hear her claim, and determine our response. The claim appears to be that she's my half-sister. My mother and Zoe respond by saying Miss Salt is a liar. Mr. Van Staden says she's a chancer without any legal status. You take the line that she's attempting a criminal fraud in order to cash in on the Villiers' money. None of you has made the smallest attempt to examine the facts in a dispassionate way, although you, Wally, have been clever enough to pretend to do so. I'm not satisfied to leave things there. I want to know who this woman is. I'm not prepared either to accept or reject her claim until there's been a full and properly-conducted investigation."

"Really, you know," Kepple's voice was less urbane, "you are merely giving Miss Salt false hopes. She admits herself she has worked for years to find proof of her identity. In my humble opinion she has failed to do so."

"That's too slick an answer. It seems to me she's produced enough evidence to justify an enquiry on a much bigger scale. By that I mean, the setting up of a committee or some such body, with funds to direct a search, the skill to sift evidence, and the authority to publish its findings."

"Complete and utter rubbish; it's not incumbent on us to finance people anxious to relieve us of our money."

"It is incumbent on us to arrive at the truth. That much is due not only to all of us here, but to my father. We gain nothing by treating Miss Salt as an enemy."

". . . My dear good boy . . ."

. . . "Matt, I want your views on this."

Matt, who had been sitting with his chin sunk on his chest,

levered himself higher in his chair. His gaze shifted from Adam to Emma Salt. He said slowly, "It's not a thing you can decide at the drop of a hat. Henry's child, born, and lost, and now perhaps alive in this room? That's something to shake up a man's mind. I don't know what's right to do. I need time to think."

"You won't get time." Van Staden spoke dryly from his corner. "Isn't it plain to you, Mr. Kinsman, that this woman is out for blood? The Furies won't wait."

Matt's regard remained fixed on Emma. "A strange night. Henry was my friend. If his child is alive, if there's a chance of that, then I want to know. Like Adam. Yes, I'd agree to a committee of enquiry. It'd have to be on certain terms, of course. Reputable members. No publicity except we were all agreed to it. We'd save a deal of nastiness if we tackled it that road."

"It's no good talking," said Emma. "I won't accept it."

"Now, don't throw out the baby with the bathwater, young woman. You can't lose by a proper enquiry."

"There won't be one."

"No," agreed Kepple, "there won't be one."

Matt turned his head lazily. "Not your decision to take, Wally boy."

"I happen to direct the Finances of Villiers Glass."

"You forget," said Adam, "that we're not discussing Villiers Glass. If Emma has any claim at all, it's on my family name and my personal bank balance."

"She has no right of access to either. I may as well tell you, Adam, while Miss Salt is here, that Mr. Van Staden and I have already discussed the legal aspects with Sir Humphrey Taggart. Naturally he is making a close study of the facts, but his immediate reaction was that Miss Salt cannot establish proof of her descent from Henry Villiers, and therefore has not the smallest right to inherit from him. Sir Humphrey also pointed out that once Henry Villiers was dead, Lisbet Villiers had the sole rights over her child. She was entitled to place it in adoption if she wished. She knew that by doing so she would deprive it of the rights of inheritance, but she chose to go ahead. Her intention was

168

perfectly clear. It follows that our own conscience is relieved of any responsibility for the child, monetary or otherwise. Morally speaking, we could not alter the course of events, and we need not concern ourselves with the resentment, nor with the financial ambitions, of Miss Salt."

"I'm grateful for Sir Humphrey's advice, but I prefer to work out my moral obligations for myself. Also the way I spend my money."

"Your money! Good God. May I remind you that what you have comes to you from Villiers Glass? What you live on is a large slice of the Company, and I'm damned if you're going to wave it about like a Salvation Army banner. It's perfectly clear that Miss Salt hopes to sink her teeth into capital and shares that don't belong to her, and if you imagine that your Board is going to sit back and watch with a smile, you are very much mistaken. And while we're on the subject of moral obligations, you might remember that you have some twelve thousand employees dependent on your decisions. Their interests won't be served if you waste Company money on a gimcrack enquiry attended, I have no doubt, by a blaze of sentimental publicity."

"It won't be sentimental, I promise," said Emma, and Kepple spun round and shook a hand at her.

"That's enough. I've given you a fair chance to get out of this without being hurt. But let me warn you that if you go to the press, if you so much as breathe a word of this to anyone, I shall make it my business to destroy you. I know how to strip you of credibility faster than you can peel a banana, and I shan't hesitate to take legal action. You'll be lucky to stay out of gaol."

"Thanks, Mr. Kepple. I'll tell the gutter press what you say. I'm sure they'll be interested."

Kepple turned his back on her. "Listen, Adam. I want one thing clear. There will be no mention of an enquiry at the Board meeting on Saturday."

For a moment the two men faced each other in silence. Then Adam said, "You're not President yet, Wally."

"And nor, my friend, are you. All you have so far is the nomination, and that may easily prove to be unacceptable to a majority of the shareholders. Don't push me too far, or I'll see you right back where you came from, with the other little boys."

"Wally." Grace's voice was hardly raised, but it stopped him in mid-flight. He glanced at her uncertainly, and she patted the sofa beside her. "Sit down, please. I have something to say."

Kepple resumed his seat. Grace, folding her hands, looked about her with gentle irony.

"It's time, I think, to make something plain; and that is, I do not propose to allow myself to be used as a pawn in a game of commercial chess. Miss Salt, you and I understand each other well enough. You consider that I wrecked your life, and you intend to wreck mine. You are at liberty to try. Like Mr. Kepple, I believe that you'll fail. I've lived in this city for a long time. During those years, I've maintained certain standards, both in my business and my private life. My reputation is reasonably secure. I've no doubt that you can and will cause me a great deal of pain and humiliation. But that is all you will do. You will not win the right to use my husband's name, and you will not get one penny of Villiers money. Most important of all, you will not dictate to me how I shall conduct my life. You may say and do what you like. It is of no account to me, and will carry no weight with people of established worth. You do not matter enough. You do not matter enough, here or anywhere else. Wally, what time is the meeting?"

"Ten o'clock."

"Good. I shall attend it, of course. I wish you to make a report to the members about Miss Salt. You will tell them as much as is necessary to show them what sort of woman she is. We will ask the Board to decide what action must be taken to defend the Company against her."

"Grace, dear, you should consider . . ."

"I have considered, Wally. Obviously we can't suppress this story. Miss Salt will not allow us to. Therefore we will fight her in the open, and we will begin at once. It may be unpleasant for a little while, but there is no doubt in my mind of the outcome. Adam, come here, please."

170

He rose and crossed to her side. Grace took his hand. "I'm glad you have the courage of your convictions, but Wally is right. You must drop this idea of an enquiry. Do I have your assurance on that?"

"I'm afraid not."

Grace stiffened. "Why?"

Adam held her gaze. "Because I must be sure in my own mind whether or not Emma is my father's child."

"Henry had only one child in the eyes of the law. You can forget this impostor." As he remained silent, her grip on his fingers tightened. "Adam. You have a duty to the Company. You have a duty to me."

He said slowly. "I know. You must let me decide what's best, in my own way."

A coldness touched her eyes. Releasing him, she said, "I can see there's no point in arguing any more tonight. We'll discuss it tomorrow. And now, I'm very tired. I am going to bed." She rose and held out a hand to the jeweller, who hurried to her side.

"Goodnight, Mr. Van Staden. I'm grateful for your presence here tonight, and your contribution to our talk."

"Not at all, ma'am. I think it has been fruitful. I'll be going back to the States tomorrow, but my lawyers will watch my interests. Get in touch with them if you need me."

Grace nodded. "Thank you. Goodnight Matt. As always, I count on your wisdom. Wally, I'll see you tomorrow. Zoe, will you come with me, please?"

She turned towards the door. Zoe put an arm round her waist and the two women moved slowly from the room.

Kepple sighed. "Well. That's that. Van Staden, can I give you a lift?"

"I'll be grateful." Van Staden stepped up to Adam. "Your mother's right, you know. In your position you can't afford sentiment. Goodnight."

He started towards the foyer, but as he passed Emma Salt, he hesitated; met her derisive gaze and hurried on. Her voice mocked him.

"Goodnight, Uncle Theo."

Kepple walked after Van Staden. Matt put out a hand

and caught his arm.

"Wally, if you're looking for trouble, you'll get it."

Kepple's smile was complacent. "I'm a peaceable man. If you want to avoid trouble, then warn Adam not to force my hand." He pulled free of Matt's grasp and went off to the elevator to join Van Staden.

Matt turned back. Adam was helping Emma Salt into her coat.

Matt said, "Don't go yet. I want to talk to you. Stay and we'll have a drink together."

Adam shook his head. "If you'll forgive me, I want to have a word with my mother before Zoe leaves."

"Yes, you go." As Adam moved away, Matt recalled him. "That enquiry. Did you draft anything?"

"Only a preliminary press release."

"Give it to me."

Adam handed over a sheet of paper. Matt carried it back to the bar counter, where Emma was already seated on a stool.

"Well, Miss Salt, what'll it be?"

"Whisky and soda, please." He poured the drinks.

"Cigarette?"

"No thanks, I'll smoke one of these." She took from her handbag a pack of the small cheroots she favoured. While she lit one, Matt scanned the paper in his hand. He looked up at last to find her watching him with steady appraisal.

"I'm going to read this to you," he said.

"It's no use."

"Shut up, lass, and listen."

He began to read:

"Dateline, January 15th.   *Daily Gazette.*

"Mr. Adam Villiers (33), Acting President of the Villiers Glass Company, yesterday told this newspaper in an exclusive interview that a woman has approached his family, claiming to be the posthumous and legitimate child of the late Mr. Henry Villiers and his wife Lisbet. (Mr. Henry Villiers died in 1939, and his widow some years later, in Nazi-occupied Holland.)

"Mr. Adam Villiers went on to say: 'I have not yet had time to consider in all its details this claim of kinship. Obviously it is a matter which must be examined with scrupulous care, both in its human and legal aspects. The implications for my family, and for the Company of which I am the acting head, are enormous.

"'It would be easy to deny at this stage any responsibility for initiating action; and to challenge the claimant to establish a case before a court of law. But I feel that such a course would lead to animosity and mistrust, and would not create the atmosphere in which we can reach a just and honest decision.

"'There is in my view sufficient evidence to make it desirable and necessary to investigate the claim with dispassion. I have therefore, in my personal capacity, and without prejudice to The Villiers Glass Company, decided to appoint a committee of three persons whose integrity and capability shall be beyond dispute, to make a thorough investigation.

"'I have further decided to create a fund to finance this project, and propose myself to donate an initial sum of ten thousand pounds (£10,000) to this fund.

"'While it is not possible at this juncture to give further details, I believe it to be in the best interests of everyone concerned to conduct this enquiry in a frank and open manner. I will accordingly inform the *Gazette* as soon as I can of the names of the committee members, and the committee's terms of reference.'"

Matt laid the paper aside. "That's a very fair offer, you know. I've no doubt that the *Gazette* would talk turkey, in exchange for exclusive rights. A paper like that could put thousands into the enquiry fund, and you'd also get payment for the story rights. With syndication, that's a big sum. The reporting would be fair, and the *Gazette*'s a paper of standing. Finally, if you accepted this, Villiers Glass could be persuaded to back it financially, and so could Theo Van Staden."

"No," said Emma.

"Why?"

"Two reasons."

"Well?"

"There's nothing more to find. I've worked for twelve years. I know."

"Omniscient? You could be wrong, even you, Emma Salt. And the other reason?"

"Time, Mr. Kinsman. An enquiry like that couldn't be mounted quickly. It would take months, years. And in that time, Kepple and Mrs. Villiers and Theo Van Staden would finish my chances. You've tried to be straight with me, so I'll be straight with you. I know there's not much chance of proving my case. There's that weak link that Kepple spotted. I know I'm speaking the truth, but I may never prove it. My one chance is to speak out now, loud and clear. Don't you see?"

"But my girl, if you act alone, you can't hope for support from reputable newspapers. A story emanating from Adam Villiers, with the Company behind him, is one thing. A story from Emma Salt, a nobody, is another. The only papers that will touch it are as Wally says, gutter rags. And Kepple will still try to wreck you, and with a much better chance of doing so than if you accepted the enquiry. Can't you trust us that far? What do you hope to gain, doing it your way? Umh? What are you after, tell me?"

Emma laughed. "Kepple's told you what I'm after."

"Money, status?"

"Once, yes. Not any more. I have enough money. I don't need their kind of status."

"Then what? A magical identity?"

She bent forward over her glass. "That's nearer. But not the way they think. I used to feel once . . . I felt I needed . . . a name. Place of my own. Right up till tonight, I believed that. I see I was wrong. What the court says doesn't matter a damn. What you people say, doesn't matter a damn. Nobody can tell me who I am, but myself."

"Then why go on? Why get hurt for some obscure revenge?"

"It's not revenge. Believe that. I must go on, that's all."

"Why?"

"Because they tried to stop me. If they'd been kind, if they'd understood what it meant to me, things might have been different. But they didn't. Long ago, those people shaped my life, Mr. Kinsman. Tonight, they tried to put the finishing touches. Emma Salt, displaced person. Mrs. Villiers said it all for me. 'You don't matter enough,' she said. 'You don't matter enough, here or anywhere else.' Well, I'm not theirs to arrange. I belong to myself. I know who I am. Going on is a part of who I am, a part of myself. You see?"

"Maybe I do." Matt reached for the whisky bottle, offered it to her. She waved it away and he poured himself a shot. "Emma, there's one other thing you must understand. If you do go on, you'll start a fight in Villiers Glass. Adam's defended you at great cost, against his friends, his mother. If he continues to take your part, Walter Kepple will use that to cheat him of the Presidency. That'll be the first move in a killing game. Adam will lose Villiers Glass."

"I've no intention of harming him. I like him all right."

"But you will harm him. Do you believe the innocent should suffer with the guilty?"

For a moment he thought he had reached her; for her mouth twitched in something almost a smile, as if at some memory. Then she shook her head.

"Adam must do what he wants."

She slid down from the bar-stool and gathered up her handbag. "I must go, Mr. Kinsman."

"Have you a car?"

"Yes."

"I'll ride down in the lift with you."

Seeing her into her car, he said, "I may want to get in touch with you in the next day or two."

She found a card in the map-pocket, scrawled a telephone number on it and gave it to him.

When she had driven off, he went back into Glass House and took the lift up to his own office floor. He found in his desk the taped record of the Holland visit that Adam had given him that morning. Carrying it through the Directors' Lounge, he played it over on the machine there. Twice he checked it and replayed a certain section.

Finally he went back to his office, locked the tape away and reached for the house phone.

He dialled, waited. A sleepy voice said, "Adam Villiers here."

"This is Matt. I'm in my office. Adam, I want to know is your mind made up?"

"Yes."

"You've no chance, laddie."

There was silence on the line, and after a moment Matt sighed. "There's one thing in your report I'd like to check. Can you take me to Heath Row?"

"Now?"

"Yes. Pettersen will have to fly me to Amsterdam. Can you get hold of him?"

"Yes, he's on standby. What are you up to, Matt?"

"I'll tell you on the way."

"Right. I'll be in the foyer in about ten minutes."

Matt replaced the receiver. From a corner cupboard he dug out the battered overnight bag he kept ready for emergencies. He switched off the lights, locked the office door, and went downstairs to wait for Adam.

XLIV

IN THE GLIMMER of an icy dawn, Mrs. Margriet Loots shook her husband awake.

"Pieter. Pieter, there's a man to see you."

Loots mumbled. "Sunday." After a moment he opened his eyes and said, "Tell him it's my day off. Who is it?"

"An Englishman called Kinsman. I never saw anyone so big and so ugly."

"Then why in God's name let him in?"

"It's snowing outside. He says it's about the Li Abas case."

Loots sat up. He looked at the clock and hissed through his teeth; rolled out of bed, pulled on a dressing-gown, went and washed his face and teeth. When he walked into the living-room, Mrs. Loots was pouring coffee and the visitor was warming himself at the fire. The Inspector took note of superfine clothing, shrewd little eyes and an air of vast, relentless purpose.

"Mr. Kinsman? What can I do for you?"

"I'm Production Manager of Villiers Glass, Inspector; a friend of Adam Villiers. He told me you were in charge of the Li Abas case?"

"That's so."

"Then you know a young woman named Emma Salt?"

"Yes. She was the little girl taken from Li Abas."

"She was. Inspector Loots, she's in London now. She claims to be the legitimate child of Henry Villiers, Adam's father; also the child placed in adoption with Alex and Susannah Van Staden."

Light glinted in Loots' eyes. He took a packet of cigarettes from the chimney-piece, lit one, and said between coughs, "Why do you come to me, sir?"

"You can say I'm acting in Adam's cause."

"No, no. I mean, why do you think I can help?"

"Maybe you can."

"The case is closed."

"I know. Did you ever consider Lisbet Jonkers' child?"

Loots grimaced. "We considered every child registered in Amsterdam between late 1939 and early 1940. Other centres too. We found no trace of the Jonkers' child; but that was a time when thousands of kids went missing. Not registered at all, sent out of the country, swallowed up in the war. You see? There is no record of the Jonkers' child from a week after it was born. It vanished from the mother's address, no-one knew where. There were sixty-nine children like that on our short list, after three years' work. So now, the case is closed."

"Could Emma Salt's story be true? Is there a chance?"

"Mr. Kinsman, I'm a policeman. I don't have to talk about chances. I need only say what I know."

"You didn't want to close it," said his wife.

"Be quiet, Margriet."

"You've often said . . ."

. . . "Margriet!"

"Mrs. Loots," said Matt, "I've not come here to put your husband in difficulties. Inspector, let me explain. In the space of the next forty-eight hours, Emma Salt is going to go to some newspaper in London and publish her life-story. She'll claim to be both Henry Villiers' daughter and the ward of the Van Stadens. Surely in those circumstances, the police must reopen their files?"

"That's not for me to say, sir. Theo Van Staden and the Gebhardts have sworn again and again there was no adoption, Alex and Susannah took no child. These are important people, you know. I can think what I like, but if I call them liars without proof, I can go out and look for another job."

"Last night," said Matt, "before witnesses, Theo Van Staden admitted that his brother did take a child; a girl about five weeks old, the daughter of Lisbet Jonkers."

As Loots stared at him with narrowed eyes, Matt leaned forward. "Were there no servants in the Van Staden household, back in 1940?"

"Several. None of them saw any child."

"Extraordinary. Were they bribed?"

"We found nothing to suggest that."

"Loyalty, then?"

"Mr. Kinsman, this wasn't that kind of family. Servants didn't like them. When we started the questions, we found not one employee who'd been with them longer than two years. If they say no child came to the house, then it's true. All we can prove is that in January 1940 Lisbet Jonkers had a daughter, and on April 2nd, Alex and his wife left Amsterdam for Java. Between . . . nothing."

"Umh." Matt set down his coffee-cup but he watched Loots carefully. "Well, I mustn't keep you here talking. Thank you for your help." He held out his hand.

Loots ignored it. "May I ask, where do you go now?"

"To Berne, to see Mina Gebhardt."

"And?"

"I plan to tell her that in two days she'll be famous."

Loots ran a fist over his tufty grey hair. "She won't see you."

"Piet," said Margriet, "you must go."

178

"No," Matt was backing towards the door, "it's not fair to ask it of you. I may use methods you can't approve."

Loots interrupted him. "You have a car?"

"A plane."

"Then we must clear flight details with the airport. But first I must call in at headquarters. Margriet, get us some food, something we can take with us. I'm going to dress, Mr. Kinsman. I won't keep you long."

XLV

THE LORINDASTRASSE IN Berne was opulent, quiet. Fifty maids with fifty mops couldn't have done a better job on the snow than the street-sweepers. Loots said, "Be careful what you say. Big money can turn nasty when it is frightened."

Matt bent to peer from his window. "I'm big money, son, and I'm frightened."

Their taxi slowed, swung between teak gates and arrived at steps flanked by squat Etruscan carvings. Matt paid the fare and followed Loots up to the door. Presently a maid conducted them to the Gebhardt drawing-room.

This was circular, and round the whole ran curtains of some thick, dun-coloured silk. No windows showed, but overhead a dome of glass admitted a syrupy yellow light. The effect was stuffy and secretive. It suited the woman who sat waiting for them.

She watched them from the far side of the room, not rising from her chair. She made Matt think of an outsize mole. She was small and plump, dressed in brown. Little spade-like hands, covered in rings, lay in her lap. Her eyes were so small as to be almost invisible between full, padded cheeks and a short, thick nose. As Loots came up to her she lifted her chin to squint up at him.

"Why do you trouble me again?"

"I have nothing to do with this, Mrs. Gebhardt. I am here to introduce Mr. Matthew Kinsman. I think when you have heard him, you will . . ."

. . . "Who are you?" She interrupted Loots with great

rudeness and switched her gaze to Matt.

"Villiers Glass," he said.

For a moment she sat quite still; then one thick fore-finger stabbed at Loots.

"Tell him to get out."

"No, Mrs. Gebhardt. Inspector Loots will remain. Perhaps, though, he wouldn't mind waiting by the door?"

Loots moved away to a distant chair. Matt chose one facing his hostess. "Your husband isn't home?"

She ignored the question. "Who sent you? Theo?"

"He knows nothing about this. I'm here to make a deal with you. It concerns the Li Abas case."

Her little feet, which hardly reached the floor, tapped in annoyance. "That is closed."

"It was." Matt's voice was soft. "Until last night. Now it's going to bust wide open. There's going to be a king-sized stink. I'm sorry for you when the press gets hold of you. You didn't play a very pretty part, did you?"

Mina Gebhardt looked straight at him. He saw that her eyes were a sort of milky brown. She said, "Who is doing this?"

"Emma Salt, the child in the Li Abas case. She claims she's the child taken by Alex and Susannah."

Relief shone in the fat woman's face. "She has no case."

"She's not going to the courts. She's going to the press. The cheap press. She's set on stirring up mud. Of course, if you charge her with libel, it will come to court. On the other hand, if you keep quiet, people will say you're afraid to challenge her. You're caught both ways."

"You don't frighten me, Mr. Kinsman. Simply, I direct my lawyers to deal with her."

"Don't fool yourself, madam. By tomorrow evening, all London will have the story of Emma Salt. By Tuesday, the world will have it, Berne included. Your neighbours and your husband's clients will enjoy the dirty details over their morning coffee."

"Why do you tell me these things?"

"Because Emma Salt also makes claims on the Villiers family. That is going to cost me money. I'm a mean man,

Mrs. Gebhardt, I don't take kindly to being skinned. So I'm here to tell you that although we can't stop Emma Salt we can do something to soften the blow."

"Pay her?"

"No, she's not open to bribery."

"Buy off the newspapers? This will cost too much."

"It wouldn't be possible. There's a better way for you and me to look after ourselves."

Her mouth pursed. "You tell me. I make no promise. I want no trouble, you understand?" She looked quickly across at Loots. "Nothing dangerous."

"No bloodshed. I agree." Matt's teeth showed in a grin. "Peace and quiet, that's what sensible folk prefer. Now. Tell me something. Tell me why you and brother Theo keep your mother at a place like Amandel? It must cost you a packet. It's sad, of course, the way she's gone, but look at it any way you like, she's more dead than alive. You could put her in a cheaper home, the State asylum. Eh? She wouldn't know the difference. Has someone got you in a half-Nelson, my dear?"

An expression of venomous fury swept over her face, and Matt laughed. "Right, aren't I? But think now. For years, you've been blackmailed. Now the secret is going to be out. Nasty for you, but it does mean you're off the hook. So why not deal with the blackmailer straight away? All you have to do is sign this. I'll fix the rest."

He fished a typed sheet from his pocket and held it out to her. She lifted it close to her face, scanned it, glanced at him over the top.

"What do you get out of it?"

"If you sign it, I can use it to break down a witness. That, I promise you, will do you and me a power of good. Emma Salt will become the concern of people who can give her what she deserves. You'll be rid of her claims. I'll save my peace of mind, shall we say, and level old debts with Henry Villiers."

The woman watched him closely. "I must first talk with my lawyers; with my brother."

"No time for that, Mrs. Gebhardt. You're used to playing

deep, aren't you? It's put you where you are now. I'm telling you, there's no way out but to gamble on me."

"Why must I trust you?"

Matt chuckled, spreading his hands. "Look at me. Can't you see I'm an honest citizen?"

Mina studied him in silence for some moments. Then she got up and pattered across the room to a desk, picked up a pen and signed the letter.

Handing it back to Matt, she said, "If there is trouble, I shall withdraw this."

Matt bowed. "We understand each other so well. I'm grateful to you, believe me. Good-day."

He strode for the door. Loots fell in beside him. Outside the garden gates, Matt checked.

"Where now?" said the Inspector.

"First to whatever authority can tell us the names of the staff employed by Mrs. Gebhardt eight years ago."

"Easy enough. And then?"

"Back to Holland. We're going to Amandel, to blackmail a blackmailer."

XLVI

IN AMANDEL, SNOW lay thin and golden under the lamps in the hospital quadrangle. Dr. Rom greeted Loots and Matt with a sort of resignation and showed them into his office.

Matt handed over Mina Gebhardt's letter. It was short, "Dear Dr. Rom," it ran, "my brother and I have decided that it is no longer necessary to maintain my mother in your hospital. We propose to move her at once to some less expensive place. I shall call on you not later than Thursday of this week, to make the arrangements. Signed, Mina Gebhardt."

Rom's face was white with anger. "This is abominable. Insulting. And you, Mr. Kinsman, why do you conspire to threaten me in this way?"

"There's no threat, doctor."

"What does Mrs. Gebhardt want?"

"She wants to save money. She doesn't need to keep her mother here any longer. She feels she's paid enough."

"Paid? It's not more than she can afford. She pays no more than any other client, and if she could pay nothing we could still keep her mother. But she can pay. She's a rich woman, rich, and mean as Judas."

"Dr. Rom, let's quit pretence. We both know that in 1940 Mr. and Mrs. Alex Van Staden took a child in adoption. We both know that Mina and Theo Van Staden preferred, for financial reasons, to conceal that fact. They were lucky. The rest of the family was dead, with the exception of their mother, who was mentally sick. She was no problem. She could be kept in seclusion, what she said didn't count as evidence. But through that very need for secrecy, Theo and Mina became vulnerable; because there was one person outside the family circle who knew the Van Staden history, and that person loved Mrs. Van Staden devotedly. Left to themselves, Theo and his sister would've shoved the old lady into a State asylum straight after the war. This person wouldn't allow that, but kept silent during the Li Abas case on the single understanding that Mrs. Van Staden was to be given the best possible treatment and care; first in a cottage in Berne, and later here at Amandel. For twenty years, Dr. Rom, the person bought security for this mad old woman. It was a sort of blackmail of love."

Rom slowly ran the creases of the letter between his fingers. "Why come to me?"

"Because if you want to help your patient, you must help me. Emma Salt is in London. You know her story?"

"Yes." Rom sighed. "She came here once."

"Tomorrow, she's going to publish the whole. All the secrets will be out, including the Van Stadens'. There'll be no more need for silence, and so our blackmailer will have no weapon. Mrs. Van Staden will be moved, unless you and I prevent it."

"Can you do that?"

"If I have the facts I need, I can put Theo and Mina in my debt. They'll do as I want."

"How can I be sure?"

"Doctor, listen to me." Matt ran a hand wearily over his forehead. "We haven't got all night. The one thing you can be sure of is that Emma Salt will do as she's promised. Once that happens, I can't help you."

"What do you want me to do?"

Matt leaned forward and took the letter from Rom's hands. "Think on these facts, doctor. One; our investigator, Phillip Boyle, mentioned casually that after the war, some old servant, not known by name, traced Mrs. Van Staden in her prison camp, and reported her whereabouts to daughter Mina Gebhardt. Two; you told Adam Villiers that in Berne Mrs. Van Staden was cared for by 'her old ayah.' That's a nurse, out East. Three; Inspector Loots told me there were no servants of long standing employed in the Amsterdam house, so it seems likely that this woman was Mrs. Van Staden's own childhood nurse. Four; the Berne authorities confirm that an elderly Eurasian woman named Hannie Schalk lived with Mrs. Van Staden in the Gebhardts' cottage until eight years ago, when they both left Switzerland to return to Holland. Five; when Adam went for an early morning walk in Amandel, he saw just such a woman climb off a bus, talk to you, and go into the hospital. I want to know, Dr. Rom, is Hannie Schalk living in this town?"

"And if she is?"

"Then I mean to show her this letter."

"But that's blackmail."

Matt leaned forward. Sweat glistened on his face and neck. "I have done nothing illegal. In two days' time, Emma Salt will have spilled the beans. The case will be reopened. Hannie will be questioned. I told Mina Gebhardt, and I'm telling you, that we can't alter that. We can only affect the way it happens. If I get the truth before midnight I may be able to buy us all a little decency. I'm not making promises, I'm offering a slender hope. That's all. Now, will you take the Inspector and me to Hannie Schalk, or must we find her by ourselves?"

Rom hesitated. Then he reached for the coat hanging over the back of his chair. "I'll take you," he said.

At twenty minutes past two, Matt put through a call to London from Amandel Police Station. On the far side of the office, Loots and Rom were in close discussion with a uniformed policeman. Outside the window, snow fell on a street straight out of a Vermeer.

Adam answered and Matt spoke briskly for some minutes. At last he said, "I'll be back as soon as I can. Start without me if I'm late. Waive the set agenda in favour of a matter of urgency, and tell Kepple to give his report on Emma Salt. Let him do that his own way. Then put your proposals for an enquiry and throw it open for debate. We can rely on Halstead to needle Wally on the legal aspects. I want you to give Wally plenty of rope. He'll try to play both ends against the middle, but don't let him. Make him come out in the open. We want him committed. All right?"

When Matt rejoined the other men, Loots greeted him with a smile. "It's good news, Mr. Kinsman. Amsterdam reports the weather is clearing. You should be able to take off this morning."

XLVII

MATT KINSMAN SHEPHERDED his two companions into the lobby of the Board Room of Glass House, and signalled them to sit down. He himself walked across to a small desk near the inner doorway; picked up the attendance register that lay there, signed it, scanned the other signatures, and laid it back in place. For some minutes he stood listening with head cocked. Someone, it sounded like Dave Hartopp, was speaking with angry insistence. A second voice cut across his, then a third. Adam's called for order.

Matt planted a thumb on the buzzer beside the door and pressed twice.

Almost at once Crowther, the Company Secretary, came out into the lobby. When he saw Matt, his face cleared. "Sir, I'm glad you're back."

Matt took the young man's arm and pulled him clear of the door. "How's it going?"

"Rough."

Matt nodded. "I'm not coming in yet. Go back. Let Adam know I'm here, but not the rest."

"You don't feel . . ."

"No. Trust your uncle. Go on."

Crowther went back into the Board Room. Matt settled himself in an armchair next to the doorway. He could hear quite clearly from there. Kepple was speaking; articulate, hurt, generous, Matt knew that tone so well. A smooth killer, Wally.

"I have said again and again, Mr. Chairman, that this woman has no case. She cannot prove any link with the Villiers family. There is that vital gap. I must ask Mr. Halstead to stop beating about the legal bush and say whether or not he agrees with me?"

Halstead spoke, mild as milk. "Really, Mr. Chairman, that is like being asked whether one has stopped beating one's wife. There's no monosyllabic answer. Let us say that while I've the greatest respect for Mr. Kepple's financial acumen, I don't accept him as a legal expert. I must talk to Miss Salt myself, and possibly ask specialist advice, before I tell this Board she has no case."

"May I point out," said Zoe's voice snappishly, "that there's no time for talking to Miss Salt or anyone else? In a few hours she'll go to the press. It's now nearly noon. We have to decide something before lunch."

"Precisely," said Kepple, "and I repeat, my proposal is that we hit Miss Salt as hard and as fast as we can. We must obtain an immediate interdict against her publishing this libel. We must also plan our own approach to the press, to discredit her in the public eye. These things are well within our powers of achievement."

"So, after all, is an enquiry," said Halstead.

"That is no answer at all." Kepple's voice was thickening now with anger. "Once we accept that Miss Salt has no case, an enquiry becomes a totally unnecessary extravagance."

"Hear, hear." (Several voices, not all.)

"I grant," Kepple went on, "that Adam has the noblest of motives. I submit, with respect, that he is also . . .
186

mistakenly idealistic."

"I'm not noble at all," said Adam calmly. "The plain fact is, I dislike your principle, and mistrust your development of the argument. I found Miss Salt truthful. Other people may find her truthful. If it appears that we have tried to suppress the truth for financial gain, the public image of the Company will suffer severely. An enquiry is just, safe, and I think expedient."

"I am glad you mention money," said Kepple sharply. "The Board must keep it clearly in mind; if Miss Salt's claim succeeds, she may greatly affect the share distribution in this Company. You agree?"

"It's a possibility one must envisage," agreed Adam.

Kepple's hand struck the table with a flat sound. "Then, sir, as head of your Finance Department, I must say this. If by the pursual of an unwarranted and in my view idiotic enquiry, the financial position of Villiers' shareholders is altered for the worse, I shall have no choice but to offer you my resignation."

Grace said urgently, "Wally, please, that is not . . ." but her voice was drowned in the rising tide of Kepple's anger.

"I don't need to say that I have the fortunes of Villiers Glass very much at heart. Resignation would mean the close of the only career I want, but I simply cannot allow myself to be party to such a massive error of judgement. One further point I must make. I'm a good deal older than you, both in years and in experience of this Company. I know the temper of the shareholders. I must warn you that if you press for an enquiry, you are likely to endanger your position as President of Villiers Glass."

"You're perfectly entitled to withdraw your support if you wish," said Adam, and Kepple lifted a hand in demurral.

"I didn't say that. I said that an unwise decision now is liable to cost you votes, not here but at the Annual General Meeting. I speak as your friend, Adam. Take the advice of older and wiser heads. Be guided by us. Drop the idea of an enquiry."

For a moment there was silence. Then Adam said, "I'm afraid I can't do that, Wally. My proposal stands. I feel

187

there's been enough debate. If the members agree, I shall now put the resolution to the vote."

Halstead said angrily, "This is unfair, Mr. Chairman. It's been made to look like a vote of confidence in you, which it is not. I must insist . . ."

Again several people burst into speech. Someone began to hammer the table. Outside in the lobby, Matt hauled himself to his feet, beckoned to the two watchers on the far side of the room, and led them into the Board Room.

XLVIII

"MY APOLOGIES, MR. CHAIRMAN."

As Matt smiled round, heads snapped towards him. Adam raised a hand in greeting and Grace said sharply, "What are those women doing here?"

Matt bowed. "With your permission, Adam, I propose to introduce them to this meeting. I believe they have information which the Board should hear before reaching its decision."

"Agreed," said Halstead promptly, and two or three voices echoed him. Adam nodded his head.

"Thank you." Matt extended a hand. "This, ladies and gentlemen, is Miss Emma Salt. Will you sit here, please?" Emma took the chair set for her, shooting an indifferent glance at the faces turned to her in curiosity, in hostility.

"And this is Mrs. Hannie Schalk."

The second woman moved more slowly to sit at Matt's right. She was old, her thin hair pulled to the top of her head in a diminutive bun. Her face was broad, the features blunt, the skin dark as old varnish. She wore a sari of white wool, a white knitted jacket. Her tiny wrists were devoid of ornaments, save for a large, cheap gunmetal watch. Her expression was at once alert and serene.

As she took her place, Matt said, "Mrs. Schalk, do you recognise anyone in this room?"

The old woman looked about her without haste. Finally she said, in the high flat voice of the Eurasian, "Mrs. Villiers

I have seen. She knew my lady, in Amsterdam."

"Anyone else?"

"No."

"I see. Now I want to ask you about something that happened a long time ago, in 1940. Can you remember?"

She gave him the half-pitying smile of one who in certain matters remembers everything for ever.

"Can you remember the brooch, Hannie?"

She nodded slowly. "Ja. There was a brooch. It came from Lisbet Jonkers."

"Tell us."

Speaking with care, choosing her words, the old woman said, "In January, Lisbet Jonkers had her child. A girl. Healthy, fine girl. She said she won't keep it, somebody else must keep it. My lady wished it for her son. For Alex. You understand? But first the baby was too small. My lady bring it to me. I keep it, look after it for one mont'. In my own house in Amsterdam. You understand?"

"Yes. You cared for the child of Lisbet Jonkers until it was five weeks old, old enough to go to Alex and Susannah Van Staden. Were you paid for this work?"

Hannie raised her brows. "Work? It was for Mrs. Van Staden, my lady."

"Yes. And the brooch?"

"Lisbet Jonkers gave it me."

"Why?"

A shrug. "She din't want it."

"Did you keep it?"

"No."

"Why not?"

"I want nothing from her. A woman who give her child away? No. The brooch was for the child."

"So?"

"When Alex was for go to Java, they tell me, pack for the child. I put the brooch inside the case."

"Can you tell us, what was it like?"

Hannie considered. "Oah, yes. Was red. And wit' a clock. A clock inside, to make go round. Nice for a child to play."

Across the table, Emma Salt stretched out her hand. On

189

the open palm lay the Kostroma replica. Hannie Schalk reached out and took it. Her thin brown fingers probed, twisted. With a small sharp click, the central boss began to revolve, throwing out shafts of fire.

"That is it," said Hannie Schalk with a smile, and held it up.

A sigh ran round the table. Zoe was the first to speak. Leaning forward, she said, "It's a trick. Obviously she's been bribed, anyone can see . . ."

But Halstead interrupted her, rising to his feet, his hand on her shoulder.

"Mr. Chairman, I take it that in view of this new evidence, Miss Salt is now ready to discuss terms for an enquiry?"

"That's right," said Emma.

"Then, sir, I feel this Board can give your proposal its undivided support. May I say how glad we are to see your confidence in yourself, and ours in you, confirmed in such a felicitous way?"

XLVIV

AT FOUR THAT afternoon, Hannie Schalk, having signed certain affidavits, went off in Halstead's care to London airport. In Adam's office, Matt spoke through the smoke of a Dutch cigar.

"Now things must take their course."

"Yes. What about the Van Stadens?"

"They won't give trouble. You've relieved 'em of a financial threat. If they step out of line, we'll twist their tails off. Have you seen your mother?"

"No. I'll talk to her tomorrow. Wally's with her now. He can help her more than I can."

"Maybe." Matt gathered up his coat. "I'm going home. I'm going to have a bath and go to bed and sleep for two days."

"Matt, I want to say . . ."

But Matt was already through the door.

Upstairs in the penthouse, Grace sat in her drawing-room. It was quiet. Sun streamed through the window. Kepple came through from the kitchen corridor, crossed to her, handed her a pill and a glass of water.

She took the medicine, swallowing quickly. "Like his father," she said. "Erratic, stubborn as a mule." She handed the glass back. "I wonder if I could have voted against him?"

"Or against me." Kepple's mouth twisted in self-mockery.

She shook her head, barely listening. "I shall refuse to see her."

"Even if she's Henry's daughter?"

"Henry? That's over, that's all done."

"Grace, listen to me." Kepple sat beside her on the sofa, taking her hand. "Nothing important is lost. We have everything we had before."

"Everything but illusion." She turned to look at him. "Poor Wally, don't you understand? Illusion was all I ever needed."

Zoe Corelli was alone. She lay fully dressed on her bed, a tumbler cradled against her chest. Sometimes she took a pull at the whisky in the glass, sometimes her lips moved as if she were busy with some calculation; but for the most part she lay still, her eyes closed, while Glass House emptied and grew quiet about her.

"Come on," said Adam.

He led the way out to the terrace. A bottle of champagne was tucked under his arm, he carried two long glasses in his hand. He set them all on the parapet. While Emma Salt watched, he released the cork and allowed some of the wine to foam over the neck to the ground.

"What's that for?" she asked.

"To placate Fortune." He filled the glasses and began to raise one towards his mouth. "Here's to you, whoever you are."

Emma looked about her; over the pinnacles of Glass House and the whorls of evening traffic, over the fat slide of the river and the still-burning stubs of factories, over all the hubs and struts and spinning spokes of outer London. She smiled at Adam and raised her glass.

"I'll drink to that," she said.